Dog Attempts to Drown Man
in Saskatoon

DOG ATTEMPTS TO DROWN MAN IN SASKATOON

DOUGLAS GLOVER

Talonbooks • Vancouver • 1985

published with the assistance of the Canada Council

Talonbooks
201 / 1019 *East Cordova Street*
Vancouver
British Columbia V6A 1M8
Canada

This book was typeset in Novarese by Pièce de Résistance
and printed in Canada by Hignell Printing Ltd.

First printing: October 1985

The stories in this book appeared originally, in somewhat different
form, in the following magazines: The *Malahat Review*, *Playgirl*, *Pierian
Spring*, *The Iowa Review*, *The University of Windsor Review*, *Fiddlehead* and
Canadian Fiction Magazine.

"Dog Attempts to Drown Man in Saskatoon" won the *Canadian
Fiction Magazine*'s annual contributor's award and appeared in 85:
Best Canadian Stories.

The author would like to thank the Canada Council and the Ontario
Arts Council for their support.

Canadian Cataloguing in Publication Data

Glover, Douglas H.
  Dog attempts to drown man in Saskatoon

ISBN 0-88922-228-2

I. Title.
PS8563.L68D6 1985   C813'.54   C85-091426-4
PR9199.3.G596D6

For Peggy Gifford

Contents

There Might Be Angels

Manuel de Cerranza de Cerranza, the fat little abbot of the cheese-making monastery at San Christobal, sniffed irritably. Shocking! Whatever was happening to the Ferrocarril? Here he was travelling first class, a noble of the church, yet sharing a compartment with a man who appeared to be a tramp.

To be sure he had not noticed at once. In the heat and confusion of the station, he had only given the man a glance. A thin rabbitty fellow about his own age clad in shabby professorial tweed. Fine. I will have an interesting conversation to pass the time to Mexico City, he had thought, and ordered the porter to stow his luggage.

Now he mused bitterly on the fallibility of first impressions. He had been hot and tired and dreading the journey through the mountains. While awaiting the arrival of the train he had day-dreamed of meeting some inspirational character, a fresh young girl, full of life and innocence, perhaps a dancer, or a professional soldier, a tough worldly man who would test him, or a Wife of Bath. Travelling by public conveyance was always a lottery. At a glance the man in tweed had seemed the answer to his wishful dreams. An eccentric intellectual, the abbot guessed. An archaeologist. A free thinker. Perhaps even an Englishman!

Well he had noticed the smell first. An acrid miasma combining stale sweat, cigarette smoke, poverty and despair billowed out from the man like a cloud. Then he noticed the threadbare condition of the suit which might have been held together by a cement of dirt. The shoes, though well-blacked, were cracked and tied with pieces of string. When the tramp shifted, de Cerranza saw more string used as suspenders and bandaid patches applied inside a dingy collarless shirt.

Yet it was the man's face he found most shocking of all. What had appeared to be thinness now looked like the outer limits of starvation. The yellowing skin was drawn tight over cheekbones and etched with a faint intaglio of dirt where there had once been lines. The eyes were large and staring and shone with a peculiar unfocussed brightness. The forehead was clear and almost diaphanous like blue-veined papyrus. The whole effect was one of utter fragility as though a breath of wind might send the entire collection of dry flesh and bones tumbling to the ground.

For his part the tramp appeared to be oblivious of his new travelling companion. While the abbot examined him, he sat with his head back against the seat as though he had not the strength to hold it upright. As the train gathered speed and left the station behind, he tilted his face to watch passively where the dun mountainsides studded with pine flashed by the window.

De Cerranza bit his thumbnail, a habit he fell into whenever he was forced by circumstances to debate with his better nature. He would, of course, prefer to travel alone rather than with this noisome hobo. He was not at all sure he could endure the smell in that close steamy compartment but he was afraid to suggest opening the window in case he offended the poor fellow. In any event he assumed the man didn't have a first-class ticket, perhaps no ticket at all. That would solve matters, he thought with satisfaction. The ticket-taker would discover the tramp and attempt to throw him off at the next station. The abbot would intercede, pay a third-class fare, and the man would travel contentedly where he belonged. That was it!

As he expected, the sound of the ticket-taker working his way along the corridor of the first-class car brought the tramp out of his exhausted revery. The tell-tale nervousness of a hobo in public exerted its influence. His eyes narrowed. He glanced sheepishly from side to side. He jammed his hands into his pockets as though afraid someone might try to steal their contents. Out of one pocket he fished a bulky sheaf of papers. He couldn't really have a ticket, the abbot thought. But it was only a set of dog-eared notebooks such as school children use, covered with a curious scribble. The tramp read a page, nodded his satisfaction, read more, and then began to read aloud in a hoarse mumble.

A door clanged shut a couple of compartments away. The tramp jumped. He glared furiously at his notebooks and tried to read again but could no longer concentrate. The abbot attempted in vain to catch his eye. The tramp surged to his feet, swaying precariously over the seated clergyman. He gulped, panic-stricken, the Adam's apple working up and down his scrawny throat. Then suddenly he slid the door open and dove into the corridor.

"Wait!" cried the abbot. "Wait! I'll help you!"

But it was no good. The tramp had mysteriously disappeared. De Cerranza peered anxiously up and down the corridor. There was only the ticket-taker emerging from the next compartment.

After giving up his ticket, the abbot sat back and composed himself for a nap. But it was soon obvious he wasn't going to get any sleep. Instead of diminishing, the pungent odour left behind by the tramp lingered and even seemed to get stronger. The compartment was on the sunny side of the train and a fierce white light blasted the abbot's eyes where he lay against the seat. Great beads of sweat coursed down his fat cheeks. He felt sick to his stomach. Gasping for breath, he fumbled with the window latch for several minutes, then flung himself down in disgust.

Anger and shame tilted against one another in his mind. Why had that awful person picked this compartment? What was wrong with him in the first place? And why was the absurd incident having such an effect on the abbot? He had a nagging feeling that he had seen the tramp before. There had been something familiar in that profile as the tramp plunged into the corridor. And of course he was ashamed that his equivocal behaviour had caused another human such anguish. Why hadn't he simply offered to help the poor fellow? Christ had mingled with lepers and prostitutes. But he, de Cerranza, preferred to work through an intermediary. Most of all he was upset because the tramp had interrupted his habitual spiritual tranquillity. Why, why, the abbot asked himself, should this ordinary business trip turn into an ordeal? Surely God had better things for him to do than to untangle frivolous moral dilemmas.

Gazing about the compartment for some distraction the abbot spied one of the tramp's notebooks which had fallen to the floor during his flight. He picked it up daintily between two fingers and held it to the light. To his surprise it appeared to be a student translation book such as he himself had filled by the dozen while at university. On the left hand, the student had copied the original Latin, on the right, his translation. With fond recollection the abbot took the book and began to read.

Again he was surprised for the translation was uncommonly true and sure. He recognized the passage, a section from Aquinas' *Isaiah*. He skimmed quickly—there was a spot he remembered well, a phrase which, due to the saints' peculiar shorthand, had troubled his translators for centuries. He happily recalled the hours spent debating this and that version with a college friend who had since become a famous and important teacher. Yes, here it was. Silvestre had always said you could tell the seriousness of a scholar by the effort he put into this phrase. And the abbot shuddered a little for the student had appended a marginal note that repeated Silvestre's argument to the word. Through some brilliant intuition he had discovered a flaw in the Latin copies and daringly altered the original itself before making the correct translation.

"That is mine," said the small hoarse voice at his shoulder. "Give it back."

The abbot had been concentrating so hard on the notebook that he had failed to notice the compartment door drawn silently aside and the tramp's sudden entry. His heart jumped and he began to puff excitedly like a startled animal.

"You frightened me."

"Give me back my book."

The tramp's voice carried a veiled threat but the abbot could see he had nothing to fear. The fellow's eyes bulged piggishly at the notebook. His body quivered with despair. He had the look of a starving man who had just had his last morsel of food snatched from his hands.

"Please, give it back."

"Come, come. I'll give you your book, but first tell me where you got it."

"It's mine. I've always had it."

"Impossible."

"I tell you it's true. I wrote those things. I don't know how."

"*Ubi sic canitur*. Do you remember that? If this is your book you must remember."

"I tell you it was a long time ago." The tramp glanced nervously about the compartment.

"Well?"

"I . . . I tell you . . . "

"I won't give back the book unless you answer me."

"It's in *Isaiah*, isn't it? I seem to remember. It means 'where thus it is sung.' It fits the context. Wait! I do remember. That's not it at all. The copyists thought that was what Thomas had written and so it was always rendered that way. Everyone mistook the shorthand. They thought the *n* was a *u* and the *v* was an *n*. And of course Thomas always misplaced the superscript *r*, making *verit-* into *itur*. He could never bring himself to move from right to left, not a fraction of an inch, to put the superscript in the right place."

"Bravo, my friend. Bravo! So what does it mean?"

"The abbreviation written correctly stood for *nisi peccaverit*."

" 'Lest he should sin'," interrupted the abbot in triumph. "I wouldn't have believed it. You must have known Silvestre, too."

"I never knew anyone called by that name."

The tramp rushed forward and tore the notebook from de Cerranza's hands. For a moment he stood glaring into the abbot's eyes, then reeled backward towards the door.

"Good God," cried the abbot. "You are Silvestre, my old friend Silvestre Quinqrix."

"I am not Silvestre. Please, leave me alone. I will go now and not bother you again."

"But it's me, Silvestre. Manolo. You must remember."

"I do not know you."

But the sound of the names seemed to weaken the tramp's resolve. At the door he halted with his hand on the latch.

"Manolo?" he questioned softly.

"Yes, yes. Let me think. I must bring you back. There must be something else. I have it. What is the significance of the date December 6, 1273?"

"Why, I remember that. Thomas had a nervous breakdown. He was at Mass that morning and had a vision. He had been working so hard that his mind could simply take no more."

"He never wrote again," continued the abbot. "Yes, you are Silvestre Quinqrix. You always said it was a nervous breakdown and I always argued that somehow on December 6 Thomas suddenly realized that nothing he had written had ever, could ever, penetrate the mystery of God."

"Manolo, Manolo," broke in the tramp, chiding gently. "Thomas was nervous and impatient. It was the sort of thing that happens to men as they approach fifty. You always used that argument as an excuse to ignore your studies."

"You're right," laughed the abbot, his face beaming. "You were so much the serious scholar. You called me a sentimentalist and said I would never be an academic. Well you were right. I am an abbot and I make cheese and I still love St. Thomas."

De Cerranza stood and embraced his old friend, kissing him on the cheek. For a brief moment he basked in the warm glow of recollected companionship. Then he stood back with his hands on the tramp's shoulders and looked carefully into his face.

To his horror the peculiar unfocussed stare had returned to Silvestre's eyes. His arms hung limp at his sides and his body trembled as though he were ready to run at any moment. Tiny bubbles of sweat erupted from the papery skin. And the odour of decay grew ever stronger in the air about him.

The abbot understood now. His friend was mad. The old Silvestre Quinqrix visited the body only infrequently. That explained his lack of resemblance; with the personality gone, the body, too, somehow began to lose its unique shape. The note-books must be all that remained of that once brilliant scholarly mind, a residuum guarded inanely by the tramp who must have attached to them the memory of lost delight.

"But what has become of you, Silvestre? Please, sit here. I won't hurt you. No, no, I won't try to take your books."

The abbot spoke soothingly and gently helped the tramp to a seat by the window.

"You are Manolo?" his friend asked uncertainly.

"Yes, Silvestre. You must remember our tiny room at the university. How we used to speak of Thomas as though he were some tutor writing down the hall. Try to remember."

"I do remember a little, but it seems to have been some other man. Now I am . . . I am . . ."

He picked vaguely at the lapels of his jacket with fleshless fingers.

"That's all right now, old friend. We can piece it together. Let me go down the corridor and find some food. That will help you."

De Cerranza heaved a sigh and stood to leave.

"Wait, Manolo, I have something to tell you."

The tramp spoke in a stage whisper full of urgency.

"Manolo . . . you were right . . . right all along. All those words . . . all those words. I am not at peace with God, Manolo." He shook his head in disbelief. "I am not at peace."

"Yes, my friend, I understand."

"My mind is like the wind; it forgets where it has been. The wind forgets."

"I will get you something to eat. Wait here, Silvestre."

"That is not important, not as important as the secret informa- tion I have to impart, Manolo. You, my old friend, must be the first to know."

"Yes?"

"I have special . . . I have seen them. They are very devious, Manolo."

"Who have you seen?"

De Cerranza spoke compassionately but he was very upset at the tack the conversation was taking. It was like talking to a ghost.

"He said, 'There might be angels.' That's what he said. So

15

devious. You cannot trust them. I am not at peace with God because of this. We have a special quarrel based on this information I have."

"Silvestre, it's not good to speak this way. Let me get you some food."

"I used to love a woman and now she's gone on a long journey perhaps to the nether world. That is why I seem so deserted, Manolo. I try to keep myself going with the secret but I cannot last any longer without her. I must go after her. But this secret I will leave behind."

At last the abbot began to understand the tragedy of Silvestre Quinqrix. The paths of the two men had parted radically soon after university. De Cerranza had waited a year or two to ponder his vocation, then had taken orders at an obscure monastery in the mountains. Meanwhile Silvestre had journeyed first to Salamanca, then the great Catholic college at Louvain. His reputation had grown. He returned to Mexico to marry and went on to produce a shelf full of books as long as a man's arm. For a time the world had waited hungrily for each new publication.

But then something happened of which de Cerranza had heard only vague rumours. There had also been a small piece in the papers. His sister had sent him the clipping. Silvestre's wife was killed in a motor accident in Mexico City. From then on there were no more books. A chance acquaintance mentioned that Silvestre still taught at the university but that he was reputed to have turned to alcohol and other women. The news saddened de Cerranza and he had been prompted to reopen correspondence with Silvestre after a lapse of several years, but he did not know what to say. He had assumed that was where matters stood. He could not conceive of such a decline as he now witnessed.

As he watched, Silvestre began to cry, screwing his face up like a little monkey.

"They are so devious, so devious. If I had only known," he burst out petulantly.

"Your wife's name, Silvestre, it was Miranda, was it not?"

"Miranda . . . yes . . . and she is gone on a long journey perhaps to the nether world. That is why I seem so deserted. I must tell you the story, Manolo. It is not long. It spans less than twenty-four hours yet it is the story of my life. Will you listen?"

"Of course, old friend. But let us have no more talk of quarrelling with God. Everything is designed for the best."

"Do not speak to me of design and what is for the best, Manuel," said the tramp bitterly. "You were always the optimist, the man of simple faith."

"Please, tell me your story, Silvestre."

For a moment the abbot was afraid the tramp would not begin, that once more he had drifted into the awful vacancy of madness. The weary starved eyes gazed out the window without focussing, as though they could see some farther landscape where pain and loss did not exist. The look brought tears to the abbot's eyes. He didn't know why. He had seen much loss and despair before. And yet somehow it seemed as though this man had lost much more, as though he had lost heaven itself.

Suddenly the tramp blinked, shuddered and began to speak in a bizarre sing-song voice.

"Once upon a time there were three angels travelling incognito on the train from Guadalajara to Mexico City."

"But, Silvestre," broke in the abbot, "this was to be the story of your life."

"Manuel," whispered the tramp, "what I tell you is the truth. I am not mad."

The vehemence of his friend's avowal warned the abbot to say no more.

"Once upon a time there were three angels travelling incognito on the train from Guadalajara to Mexico City. One was pretending to be a businessman. The second a university professor travelling with his wife. And the third had taken the guise of an ignorant peasant. Of course you must know, Manolo, that angels always travel incognito. It is a cardinal rule in Paradise that since angels are instruments of grace their goodness must be wholly secret and not necessarily deserved.

"At any rate the three angels began to talk to each other the way angels will when they think they have a typically wayward human within talking range. And as you would expect they were good according to the roles they had chosen for their earthly incarnations. The professor demonstrated great intellectual virtues and produced many valid arguments for the existence of God in a way that would inspire faith in the others. The businessman demonstrated great practical virtues and told his listeners that God helps those who help themselves. And the peasant angel, well he smiled agreeably and laughed and winked at the professor's wife who was getting bored.

"However, as soon as there was a pause in the conversation, this peasant piped up in all innocence, 'Well, masters, I myself think that after all is said and done there might be angels.' Now, Manolo, you must understand that this is where the deviousness comes in. This particular angel was extremely sly. He knew that this was just the sort of ingenuous remark a peasant might make in such exalted company. At the same time it completely put the others off the scent as far as his true identity was concerned. After all no angel would for a moment entertain publicly the notion that angels exist.

"Well as you can imagine there was a heated discussion between the professor and the businessman on the impossibility of angels. The professor explained that belief in angels was a holdover from the ancient pantheistic cults. The businessman wanted to know how anything could exist without a body. As he said, to the practical man it made no sense to talk about something that wasn't in any particular place.

"The wife yawned. The peasant laughed and rolled his eyes. As the debate between the professor and the businessman became more heated, he took out a coin and did some clever business with his fingers, making the coin dance and hop over his knuckles, disappear into his mouth and come out his ear, and so on. By the time they reached Mexico City, the professor and the businessman were exhausted and the wife was smiling a private little smile as women sometimes do.

"In the confusion at the platform, the professor dropped a small book of popular theology on the seat where the peasant could not miss it. The businessman slipped some bills into the simple fellow's coat pocket. And while they were at it the peasant pinched the professor's wife and picked the businessman's pocket."

At this point the tramp hesitated. In telling the story his whole

18

demeanour had altered. It was as if from the depths of his being some new energy had come forth to animate his soul, the final sprint of an exhausted runner as he nears the finish line. His hands moved to illustrate the plot. His eyes rolled and twinkled to show how the peasant had carried on. It gave the abbot the impression of an actor or professional comic going over some well-rehearsed piece. Yet now the energy seemed to fade like the lights blinking in a house during a storm. For a moment the tramp slipped back into his fatigue and despair. Once or twice he opened his mouth to speak but nothing came out but a hollow click.

"Silvestre, Silvestre," encouraged the abbot. "Shall I get you something to eat now? Come, we can finish our talk when you have more strength."

The tramp looked wildly into the abbot's face. He strove violently to go on. His arms thrashed a little. His face began to turn purple. Specks of foam showed on his lips. The abbot placed a hand on his arm to quiet him.

"I . . . I must tell you now."

"Yes, yes, my friend. Just rest a moment."

"The woman, Manolo, she had been married to the good professor, or the man she thought was a good professor, for many years. To tell the truth, for a spirited woman like that it was a little stifling. As you humans will do, she began to doubt the existence of God simply because her husband was such a good and faithful servant. It is something that happens."

"I understand, Silvestre."

"That jolly peasant made her laugh, Manolo. Of course, he was rude. But he reminded her of the taste of life which she had missed for so long. And that evening she got down on her knees for the first time in many years and thanked God for being alive. The next day, in a state of grace, she was run over by a bus and taken to Paradise."

The tramp suddenly stopped and fell back in his seat as though dead. The abbot leaned close and felt his wrist to reassure himself that life went on inside the still body. Then, instead of letting go the emaciated hand, he held on tightly.

It seemed to the abbot that in all his years as a humble monk in the monastery he had never seen a human soul in such torment.

Compared to Silvestre, he had spent a life of blissful contentment, glorifying God in solitude, doing his humble work. Never
had he been tested. Never had he been called upon to define
his faith. Now with all his heart he wanted to save this poor soul
from the suffering and madness into which it had fallen.

He tried to think of something to say. All that came to mind
were the comforting clichés and formulae he had used all his life.
He realized with a feeling close to panic that none of them applied.
There was nothing he, as a man of God, could do for Silvestre.
Nothing. In the silence of the train compartment swaying through
space and time he held onto the hand of the other as though
the hand and the hand alone were all that kept the weary soul
from spinning off into the cold and infinite night.

At length, the tramp stirred.

"Silvestre," whispered the abbot, "can you hear me?" The
words came haltingly, with many pauses, like the steps of a man
feeling his way in the dark. "It is Manolo, your friend. I have come
for you, old man. It is time."

"Manolo? I don't understand."

"The Archangel has sent me to bring you back."

"The Archangel?"

"Who else? We were very angry at first, Silvestre. It had never
been done before, this abandoning of one's project. But the
Angelic Tribunal agreed that the peasant had not acted fairly.
I myself pleaded your case, Silvestre. And Miranda was at my
side."

"Miranda?"

"Yes, of course. Do you think she had forgotten you? Why only
this morning . . . but that can wait until you see her yourself."

"Miranda?"

"Well, come on now. You must get something to eat. It's not
quite time yet. Tomorrow we'll be off. Do you feel strong enough
to walk?"

"Yes, Manolo. Did you say tomorrow?"

Shortly afterward the train arrived in Mexico City. The fat little
abbot supported the tramp to a taxi and took him to a nearby
hotel where he collapsed for the final time. A doctor was called
immediately and the case explained to him, but there was nothing

20

he could do. The abbot watched quietly by the bed through the night lest his friend should wake and find himself in strange surroundings.

Chuck Waunch Is Dead

The goat-kid skeleton in the Peruvian leather pouch hanging above his bed is for luck. A gift from Eugene. In Annie's room down the hall Willie Nelson and Waylon Jennings sing *Mama, Don't Let Your Babies Grow Up To Be Cowboys* on the radio. In the bathroom the shower is running. Teri, washing her hair, sponging the make-up from her face, irrigating the dry residue of sex with her gangster friend whom she has earlier bundled out the front door with bored apologies. Teri, singing. A hymn. The gangster of the petty variety. A man who sells lottery tickets. He: Philip: staring at shards of coloured glass suspended before a window where they turn unhurriedly in the morning sunlight. His finger marks a page in a paperback edition of Rilke's *Malte Laurids Brigge*.

Sunday.

Hair dryer. Tammy Wynette. Hank Snow. Bathroom door. "Poetry is not, as people imagine, merely feelings (these come soon enough); it is experiences." Teri's heels hammer the carpetted stairs. The front door slams. She is off to the corner store past the Estonian Church on Broadview for eggs, orange juice, muffin mix, the *Star*, and the *Sun*. A weekly expiatory ritual. Teri makes up for her sins—her inability to hold a job, to pay her share of the rent, to stem the nightly march-past of strange men— by her cheerful willingness to perform unnecessary household chores. The news comes on. With a groan Annie switches the radio off. He can hear her muttering to the cats, Otto and Solange, both neutered. Bedroom door. Bathroom door. She sighs as she eases herself onto the toilet seat. Sighs. Urinates. Annie's gross intimacy has a way of discounting his presence. By ignoring it. She stalks naked from her bedroom to the bathroom. Fat-thighed Venus. Snapping her hair back like whips. She has a self-contentment which men translate as mystery. For Philip it is all bodily function: humid, claustral, repugnant. Observed by Philip she remains secret. Like her cats, his gender is without threat. Is this because he is her brother, or because of his homosexuality?

Messages.

The shower runs. Front door opens. Telephone rings. He hears Teri answer. The first of the Sunday phone calls. The parents calling from Sudbury. An older sister calling from Kleinburg. The maiden aunts in Willowdale. Rick, Teri's former fiancé, all the way from Chicago. Dave, Annie's ex-lover calling from Chinatown. Assorted male voices requiring dates. This is their first weekend in the apartment in over a month. The three of them have been staying at the family cottage at Wanapitei, living off Annie's charge cards and Rick's benevolence. The Rilke is Annie's, a gift from a writer friend she dropped just before the holiday. The book was left by mistake when they took the train north from Union Station. Now he is reading it because he feels sorry for the writer and knows that Annie has no interest. Sometimes Philip regards himself as a receiver of messages meant for other people.

On the train we met a childhood friend of Annie's who dragged us to the bar car to hear her stories of husbands and lovers. Several Black Russians later Annie received a note from a man

24

who wrote that she was "one hell of a woman." Annie stood on her seat and yelled out the man's name but the man didn't have the courage to declare himself in public. The women shrieked; they made jokes with the bartender. Every man in the car was intimidated. When the women went to the bathroom, the man who had sent the note introduced himself to me and then hurried out of the bar. He seemed older than I had expected, almost middle-aged. He was tall and paunchy and carried a travel-worn sample case. His suit was rumpled as though he had slept in it. His breath was bad. I shook his hand, holding it a split second longer than necessary. The man's eyes shifted with embarrassment. He was wearing a wedding band. He seemed almost grateful when I finally let him go, as though through desire he had suddenly strayed across some alien frontier and had found himself in jeopardy. When Annie returned, I gave her the man's phone number and urged her to call him when she came back to the city. We all understood that it was the combination of Annie's striking face which, like a mask, gave nothing away and her fat thighs that made her interesting to this kind of man. "I am a specimen for a trophy case," she once said. "No one will ever love me." But on the train we merely laughed. Annie refusing to let me identify her admirer.

Eugene will not call.

Teri's head appears in the stairwell as she delivers the first invitation of the day. The maiden aunts would like the three of them to appear for tea at about 4 p.m. Annie sighs once more. "There goes my afternoon nap." Teri laughs. Mary Rose, the Kleinburg sister, is bringing her two daughters. A cause for relief. And anxiety. Teri and Annie will be able to play with the youngsters while Mary Rose makes adult chit-chat with the aunts. No one expects Philip to do anything but brood politely. But the presence of Mary Rose is also a burden. "Will Gary be there?" asks Annie. He being the husband. Gary travels; he sells sunglasses. He drinks too much and, as Annie says, "He likes women who look like whores." This amuses Philip because he knows that Annie is Gary's favourite sister-in-law. Intuitively Gary is drawn by the sluttishness of fat thighs and the mask-like face. He doesn't, of course, know about the lacy camisoles and the crotch-high black leather boots hidden in Annie's room, but he senses them. Mary Rose has been on the brink of divorce for three years; she hesitates because of the children and because she is afraid she will never find another man. On a whim Annie and Teri took her to the wine bar at the Ports to show her that she was still attractive. "Toronto is depraved," she said. But later Annie told Philip their sister was secretly pleased at the attention she received from men younger than herself. Annie and Teri want her to divorce Gary because they find him odious, yet they are also disturbed by the prospect. Philip has watched them playing with Mary Rose's babies; it is a role they adopt with grace and humour. To them marriage and family represent a positive image of happiness. Yet they also crave certainty; and they see their certainty foundering in Mary Rose. Annie has her "terrors." Teri has her crying jags. The two sisters have lived together for five years. Since Annie broke up with Dave. Philip notices how year by year they grow to resemble the maiden aunts whom they affect to treat as mannish caricatures.

Annie's "terrors."

Anhedonia, or the inability to experience pleasure.

Philip walks to the bathroom in his underwear. Stops at Annie's door. She—on the bed brushing her hair, staring at nothing. The barnboard bookshelves Dave made now askew for want of bracing. The abalone shell pheasant he brought from Hong Kong hanging on the wall. "It's genuine folk art," Annie says defensively. Floral calendar with the days of her period marked in red Xs. Dingy sheets. Bulletin board with an invitation to a poetry reading and two guest passes to a Grey Cup party two years out of date. In the corner a rattan throne bought at an import shop. By the bed a candle for love-making almost burned to its holder. He wonders where she keeps the boots which she bought on a whim and which were too small for her feet. To Philip there is something touching about this. Annie prides herself on self-control. The boots

26

were an adventure, a tiny step across a border into the province of her unacknowledged self. Immediately she was embarrassed. She cannot wear them; neither can she get rid of them. Annie is a trapeze artist. Swinging.

Will she return to the platform? Will the man catch her? Will she let go? Will the net break her fall?

There is no net.

It was Rick who told us about the boy on the Matchless motorcycle who took care of the empty cottages over the winter and did maintenance chores throughout the summer. He had been hired the year before by Rick's father and several of the wealthier cottage-owners, who also happened to be Americans. Snowmobiles had suddenly made the lake accessible during the off-season and the cottagers were worried about vandalism. The way Rick's father met the boy was notable. He and some other men had been shooting clay pigeons at the gun club when the Matchless spun to a halt in a whirl of dust in the club parking lot. The boy, dressed in greasy jeans, a T-shirt and cracked biker boots (no helmet) watched as the men shot a round. Then Rick's father walked over and asked him politely what he wanted. The boy asked him if they shot for money. "Sometimes, yes," said Rick's father, who had been shooting for years and had badges and trophies for marksmanship. The boy had an old breech-loading single-shot 12-gauge in a saddle holster; he bet Rick's father $50 a pigeon. A third man held their money while the boy and Rick's father shot. At first they matched each other target for target. A little over-confident, Rick's father missed his third. He knew he would make it up on the doubles because the boy had only one shot. But the boy was lucky—when the clay birds came out high and low together he waited until they crossed and took them both at once. Rick's father missed another single. When the next double came up, Rick's father said, "Double or nothing you can't do it again." The boy shot once, smashing the high bird and winging the low so that it snapped neatly in half but did not shatter. When the round was over Rick's father owed him $300. After

27

declining to shoot again, the boy collected his spent shells and his money and rode back down the bushroad to the highway. Later Rick's father saw the motorcycle outside a diner and went in to offer the boy a job. When the boy said he would think about it, Rick's father offered to give him a $2,000-gun to spice the deal. The boy said he would think about it. And the day before Rick's father left for home, the boy rolled up the drive on his bike and took the job. But not the gun.

Ironies.

First there was the irony of his name. Chuck Waunch. Beneath the sleeve of his T-shirt he wore a dagger tattoo with the words FREEDOM OR DEATH. He walked with a slight limp and his nose had been broken. Chuck Waunch. Not Charles. In this way reality is always cancelling mythology. Then there was the irony involved in his hiring. The cottagers, represented by Rick's father, respected him because he beat them. But shooting was only a game. In real life their superiority was founded on nationality and family fortunes. They tried to buy Chuck Waunch; Rick's father had money in sporting goods—that $2,000-gun was a write-off. Chuck took the job but remained unbought. An obsolete dignity. Again there was the irony of the telling. Rick's irony. On the one hand because he enjoyed seeing his father beaten. On the other hand because, by extension, he had been bested as well. So he made his father out to be an emasculated boob and Chuck a Hemingway caricature, an impossible yokel-Hercules. The truth being that Rick's only talent was parody and that he had wasted his life and his chances with Teri. The irony of our listening. I recall that it was about 1 p.m. and we were not sober. Floating by the dock on air mattresses. Foster Grants. Lobster flesh. Wine in the cooler. Rick droning among the deer flies. Laughter bouncing off the wavelets like light. "A poseur," said Rick. "A veritable poseur. I peeked in his saddlebags one day—he carries a library in there. Kierkegaard and Nietzsche and William Carlos Williams. Saturday nights he plays jazz cornet with the band at the lodge. He lives in a tent." "How old is he?" I asked. "Twenty-two or twenty-three, maybe. No one knows." "Where did he come from?'' asked Teri, trying to place him among the various types she had known growing up in Sudbury. '' 'Up north','' mimicked Rick, jerking his thumb. ''That's all he says. Dad got so mad at him. 'Where you from, boy?' 'Up north.' 'Where up north, boy? Cochrane? Sioux Lookout? Churchill? Tuktoyaktuk? Where, boy?' It drives him crazy. He's always trying to beat Chuck down.'' Teri laughed tolerantly. Now that she no longer thought she was in love with Rick, his wit had lost its bite. ''When are we going to meet this BABY?'' demanded Annie languidly. ''Yes, when?'' I echoed. Our capacity for boredom was limitless. Even our curiosity was ninety percent boredom. ''Sick, sick, sick,'' said Teri. ''You're like the nobles of France going to watch the idiots drool.'' Annie and I got the giggles; I have said we were not sober. And of course the irony was that the story of Chuck Waunch made us ineffably sad like waking from a pleasant dream one can no longer recall. We were all looking for heroes without ever wanting to find one.

The second to last irony was Chuck falling in love with Teri.

There is no net.

Downstairs. Kitchen. Sun porch to the rear where the cats' litter boxes are kept. Odours of cat manure, coffee, muffins and Annie's Matinees. ''These muffins are FUCKED UP,'' she says, holding the smoking pan with a dish towel. She looks blowsy in her dressing gown, her face plump with sleep. ''That was Mary Rose,'' says Teri, hanging up the phone. ''She says Gary's not coming. He just got in from a week in California and he's tired out from all the Holiday Inn waitresses he met.'' The sight of Annie chipping muffin remains from the pan doesn't diminish her animation. ''She wanted us to get our stories straight for this afternoon.'' The sisters make plans over coffee. The family conspiracy. They derive from a clan noted simultaneously for gossip and secrecy. No one must know, for example, about Mary Rose's problems with Gary. These are easier to conceal when Gary is not present. Victor, Teri's gangster, becomes an entertainment marketing executive. The holiday was uneventful. Teri flirted with her old boyfriend Rick and was courted by a local fellow too rural for words. A gust of laughter follows Teri's suggestion that they tell the aunts she and Philip are thinking of incorporating as a party catering service; the truth being that they are both unemployed. Since she left Dave, they will say, Annie has been waiting for her white knight though they are worried about where to keep his horse once he arrives.

When Annie becomes involved with a man she spends all of her spare time thinking, "This is something I can get out of in a week, or a month."

Eugene had said to him, "You frighten me. You always seem coiled and ready to strike."

Teresa.

"Victor is going to find me a job," she says. "In a restaurant his brother owns." Sunday mornings she is the conversational motor. "We were the first family on our street with an indoor toilet," she says, trying to interest them in a game of reminiscences. Annie pours muffin mix into the clean pan. Philip prints in pencil on the grocery pad: BUT IT IS NOT ENOUGH TO HAVE MEMORIES. ONE MUST BE ABLE TO FORGET THEM AND HAVE VAST PATIENCE UNTIL THEY COME AGAIN. (RILKE) The pencil point snaps because he is pressing too hard. "Her family was definitely union while ours was always management," says Teri who has a habit of expressing herself in categorical statements. She loves Travis McGee mysteries and Jeanette Mac-donald movies on the Late Show. "When I was ten I suddenly realized not everyone was Catholic. I cried and cried for them," she says. The others are silent; Teri beats on against the current of their indifference. "The truth is I don't know anything now I didn't know when I was six." She has always wanted to be an entertainer. In high school she won praise for her portrayal of a lunatic in *Marat/Sade*. (Which is how she knows about French nobles and idiots.) In conversation she dangles Hollywood tid-bits culled from the book *Hollywood Babylon* and *People* magazine.

When Rick proposed, he offered to buy a club in Evanston where she could produce her own cabaret show. That night, for the first time, she slept with another man. "I wanted to see what I would be missing," she said, signalling her preference for a life of possibility, of daydream and fantasy. She still performs, although her audience is serial; Annie calls them her "little frennies," the one night stands picked up at Brandy's or Bemelman's. On the job Teri is adept at creating office soap operas which result in resignation or dismissal. "I want things to be dramatic," she says. Annoyed when the rent comes due, Annie will say, "Teri could make a Peyton Place out of the Vatican."

Which is not the whole story, thinks Philip, who sees them all as aspects rather than individuals. From his own experience he knows that Teri is only passing time, that she is waiting, on the alert for something mislaid, abandoned or forgotten. Yet familiar.

He remembers their mother, a surgical nurse, brushing her hair before pressing it into a hygienic bun. Her hair being her single vanity.

He remembers the mysterious glow of the slag heaps on a summer night.

He remembers making ghost faces with a flashlight in order to frighten the little girls, Annie and Teri.

The phone rings. Who has not yet called?

Sundays at Wanapitei our parents would drive from Sudbury to take the women to Mass. In preparation for the Sabbath pilgrims, Rick would arrive early with his boat. The two of us would then escape across the lake, sometimes stopping in full view of the cottage to take drugs and lounge naked in the sun. Serving tea on the cedar deck, Annie and Teri would be inexplicably vague as to my whereabouts.

Evenings Rick came for us and we would criss-cross the lake

in search of parties, splitting the black water like a zipper open-ing. Once, already drunk, we stopped the engine far from shore, snorted cocaine and were caught in a violent thunderstorm. We were silent with terror and shock for what seemed minutes but could not have been more than a few seconds. The thunderclaps seemed to vibrate in my breast bone. I stared wildly about, my eyes refusing to close, to shut out the explosions of light. And then Teri said, quite casually, "This is RIDICULOUS. My mascara's running." Annie began to laugh, an unnaturally high-pitched out-burst that took us by surprise. I saw her pale face upraised to the lightning. A vein pulsing near the corner of her eye. She was weeping as well as laughing. Suddenly we were all laughing.

At the cottage I picked up a glass to pour myself a drink. The glass shattered in my hand either because it had been cracked earlier or because my grip was too strong.

Saturday night the four of us drove to the lodge in Rick's car. There was a line-up outside. The man in front of us said, "I come from Toronto every weekend to hear this guy. This guy plays like a 90-year-old nigger." We heard the opening of the first set through the door. *Summertime*. Played sad and low, yet with such power that it seemed to resonate in the surrounding forest and return a hundred times before the sound died. Holding Annie's hand, I felt her shiver. The man in front of us turned and said, "Like a 90-year-old BLIND nigger."

We were seated at the break.

The cornet player was leaning against a piano, a cigarette and a glass in one hand, picking out notes with the other, ignoring the audience. He wore a T-shirt and jeans, the way Rick had described him. But he was thinner than I had imagined, skinny. His head and hands seemed too big for the rest of him. And his eyes were a startling blue-white like the inside of an oyster shell. For an instant I thought he really was blind; he had that look. His shirt was soaked with sweat.

There was a common intake of breath as he began to play the second set. Conversations dangled. The waitresses huddled at the end of the bar. The first note, at the end of a long interval of silence, was like a climax that built and built in waves of sound. *Summertime* again. His signature tune. This time hot and sultry. Full of erotic innuendo. As though he was bent on erasing the implied sorrow of the first version. Then right into something up-tempo that I didn't recognize. A medley of tunes, getting wilder, stronger, meaner. The rest of the group, alto sax, bass and drums, hung back at first, put under a spell of awe by the horn man. Then, emboldened, they took up the invitation, followed his lead, played over their heads. After a few bars I could see the surprise in their faces. He was making them look good, teaching the riffs and bridges as they went along, breaking in when they began to falter. Faster and faster he played, changing direction every other note, impatient and exasperated, straining to squeeze more sound out of the instrument than seemed humanly possible. And then, suddenly, *Summertime*, a reprise. He blew us a vision of it. Waving the others off, he blew the last bars alone, each note a recovery of that mysterious past which is continually eluding us like sunlight shimmering before the bow.

Afterward Teri could not take her eyes off Chuck Waunch. She was suddenly furious with Rick and sent him away saying, "You're always hanging around. You make me so damn nervous. Why can't you leave me alone?" But when he got up to leave, she took his arm, refusing to let him go. Outside Rick pointed to the Matchless gleaming in the moonlight against the trees at the edge of the parking lot. We waited for perhaps an hour, expecting its owner to appear at any moment. The parking lot cleared; lights in the lodge began to go out. Then, quite suddenly, though it did not seem to surprise us, we heard the bell-like tones of the cornet. Judging from the sound of it, he was standing about a hundred yards from us, by the lakeshore. We could still hear him, far away across the water, when we finally reached the cottage.

She was so shy when she met him that all she could think of was Rick's father. "Where you from, boy?" "Up north," said Chuck, jerking his thumb. "Where up north?" she asked. "Cochrane? Sioux Lookout? Churchill? Tuktoyaktuk? Where, boy?" He took her for a run on the motorcycle. They hit a hundred miles an hour on the way from Wanapitei to Hanmer where the road was rough. When they came back, they were laughing because her finger-nails had dug bloody half-moons in his chest. Her eyes were full of strangeness. And after he had gone she cried for an hour in Annie's arms. "I thought we were going to DIE," she said. "There wasn't any reason NOT TO."

Stoned on Rick's hashish, Annie tapped her forehead and said, "I think our little Teri has finally bitten off more than she can screw."

Eugene will not call.

The goat-kid skeleton in the Peruvian leather pouch hanging above his bed is for luck. A gift from Eugene.

The jar of vaseline on the night table used to repel Annie.

When the sisters bicker Teri always draws attention to Annie's dirty fingernails, the mounds of cigarette ash on the carpet, and her morning cough.

Eugene keeps pigeons in his attic and collects antique bric-a-brac such as brass buttons, Japanese fans, and German *fayreings*. His last words to Philip were: "I'm not going to give you a break this time. Everybody gives you a break—that's your trouble." As usual it was an argument about infidelity. And as usual Eugene failed to realize that the sexual *la ronde* held no intrinsic interest for Philip but served; along with drugs, as a distraction.

One Halloween he had been arrested having escaped from a Cabbagetown party in nothing but a sequined G-string. His explanation: "I took too much something-or-other."

Their mother is on the phone. Philip retreats to his bedroom

34

to avoid the shrilling voices. From the sounds that Annie is making he judges that his mother already knows about tea with the maiden aunts. The family conspiracy again. This time the girls and their mother against the mother's sisters. Marrying Bob, their father, a Protestant telephone company lineman, she had married down. A source of tension in the extended family. On the other hand she had produced offspring, giving her somewhat of an edge on her barren sisters. And of course there was the ever-present possibility of redemptive conversion. Bob's father, a crusty Scottish-Presbyterian, had taken a special liking to his daughter-in-law and it was whispered in family conclaves that on his deathbed he had asked her to bring him a priest. "We get them all in the end," says Annie. Philip, who sees things somewhat differently, says, "It's rather sad; all those lifelong doubters losing their courage." "Maybe they find it," says Annie.

In the bathroom he takes four aspirin washed down with water sipped from a cupped hand. Replacing the aspirin bottle he dislodges a precariously stacked ledge-full of makeup kits, deodorant bottles, pill cases, shampoo tubes, tweezers, nail clippers and perfume samples. Something green and viscid oozes from a cracked container down the sink drain. Philip returns to his bedroom. A fly circles the ceiling, occasionally striking the globe light fixture with a musical ping. The fly increases Philip's sense of being out of control. He stares at the glass mobile. Rubs his eyes. Runs his hands through his hair. In two weeks his unemployment benefits will stop. He is uncertain what he will do after that. It was Eugene, actually, who knew the ins and outs of specialty baking; Philip was only his helper. His work experience includes apartment superintendent, sales clerk in a gay bookstore and night-watchman. For three years before that he was in the seminary. He still wears black. His jeans are dyed black, his T-shirts. Occasionally he has made money going with men who look much like the man on the train who wanted to meet his sister.

"Muffins," calls Teri on the stairs. Her voice is cheerful mixed with a grain of sisterly concern. "She's off the phone."

He remembers Annie's rules for handling men:

1) Never apologize.
2) Never explain.
3) Never give second chances.
4) Never phone them.
5) Never make a clean break;
   always keep them guessing.

Descending the stairs he smells muffins, strip bacon, fried tomatoes and scrambled eggs. Even though he knows there are only muffins. The rest is from childhood.

Landscapes.

It was difficult to resist the temptation to imbue the chemical wasteland that surrounded Sudbury with symbolic values. Yet to have grown up there was to believe at some level that everything man touches dies. At Wanapitei the lake was eutrophying due to the proliferation of cottages and septic tanks. I was present when Chuck Waunch showed Teri where the conifers had been burned by acid rain. That summer it seemed as if there was more decay than usual. Not just natural decay but something induced and hyperactivated, a subliminal hastening of last things that rustled among the dead leaves and undergrowth like a wind. Writing this I know that I was guilty of the fallacy of superimposing the arid substance of my own ego onto the landscape as though there were some necessary connection between the two. But I felt the connection.

From the beginning Annie and I saw the maintenance man as a threat. Chuck Waunch had brought us to the borderlands. On mornings when Teri returned, her lips bruised with love-making, it seemed possible that she would be tempted to leave us. Outwardly we remained indifferent though a note of cunning invaded our conversation. Our afternoon languors on the lake turned into debates, our debates into elaborate shadow-games which betrayed anxiety without betraying the one who was anxious.

"Are you and your new little frennie planning to live in a TENT?"
"Honestly, Teri, how can you expect a man with FREEDOM OR
DEATH tattooed on his bicep to learn to take out the garbage?"
"Looking down the road, I think the question we have to ask
ourselves is whether or not Chuck Waunch is executive material."

This was what Annie called "riding it out."

Those days Teri was uncharacteristically quiet. She seemed
almost embarrassed by her new attachment, as though, when he
was not present, she had difficulty believing in him. Usually she
accepted a certain amount of good-natured ribbing about her
boyfriends. But now she felt the need to defend Chuck. "The others
were bright, amusing, kind—they got my jokes—but him, he opens
me up. I've never felt this way before." Whenever Teri became
defensive, Annie would adopt the tone of an older, wiser sister.
"If you're serious about this man, why not ask him to move to
Toronto so that you can date him a while before rushing into things.
A few months won't make a difference if he really loves you."
Sometimes, exasperated, she would appear to lose patience. "Just
remember to take your damn pills, Teri. We don't want you showing
up next spring with a little present from Chuckie." And sometimes
she would be cynical. "Nothing is forever, sweetheart. Look at
Mary Rose and Gary. You can always get a divorce."

Contradictions.

The contradictions were within us. We wanted her to go. We
admired Chuck Waunch. Once Rick said, "He's a cliché. Self-
consciousness is simply not in his repertoire." Annie turned on
him angrily. "Not all of us were born rich enough to make a pro-
fession out of going to parties. If you mean he actually DOES things
instead of sitting on his ass endlessly passing ironic commentary,
you're right." This remark was unfair and somewhat heavy-handed.
After all, we went to the same parties. But it showed how deeply
split Annie was in her feelings toward Teri's lover. Yet when Teri
came to her, her counsels remained guarded and ambiguous.
"Love is a matter of luck," she said. "I have had friends tell me,

'I know we're going to have to work at it.' I always think they're wrong. The real thing requires no effort." And when Teri turned indecisive—"It's so difficult!" she cried—instead of offering reassurance I took her hand and said, "If you leave, who will I have to talk to?"

"Let's wait and see," she told him. Her relief was evident. Unexpectedly, since lost love makes lawyers of us all, he offered no protest. She talked of finding him a new job for the winter but he stolidly refused to consider moving to the city. As long as the weather held, he said, he would ride down on the Matchless. Meanwhile we had decided to leave early for Toronto.

On the last night Chuck Waunch came to the cottage to say goodbye. Instead of stopping inside for a drink he led Teri away along the shore. "I watched the wolf die here," he said, gesturing into the lake. She had heard the story before—how he had watched a party of deer hunters on snowmobiles harry a dog-wolf to death on the ice. "They had cut him in two. From the ribs back he was butcher's meat. His guts hung out like ropes and bags. When he saw me he jumped on his forelegs and ran, dragging the rest behind. I went after him with an axe but every time I got close he would jump up and run. Until I got sick of it and left him alone. He was only a few yards from me and I could hear him spitting and snarling, grinding up the snow crust with his teeth. I nearly froze waiting for him to die. It was a stupid thing to do but I was ashamed of having chased him." They made love on a blanket like moths beating against a light; he held her by the throat when she came. Afterwards they swam and watched a bat hunting. "I rented a cabin near Hanmer," he said, "where we could be alone." "Let's wait," she answered. "It's not the best time. It'll make a mess." "Don't think about it. Just come. You don't have to go home so soon." She swam away from him in fear. "I've made plans," she said. "Everyone would know about it." It was more difficult than she had expected. The thought of him getting the cabin ready for her made her want to cry. "I'm so confused." "Just come." Treading water in the darkness she thought of the wolf.

"They always try to change you," said Annie as the train swept south out of the forest. "I've never met a man who didn't think he had the key." "Allegory is an outmoded art form," I said. It was the sort of thing I often said and I knew that because I could say it I would never be a poet. Privately, I imagined to myself that Chuck Waunch had mistaken Teri's superficiality for stoicism, her detachment for wisdom. She was the romantic sufferer men were always falling for. In the end everyone tries to find something in his lover that isn't there.

"BUT IT IS NOT ENOUGH TO HAVE MEMORIES. ONE MUST BE ABLE TO FORGET THEM AND HAVE VAST PATIENCE UNTIL THEY COME AGAIN. (RILKE)" Annie reading his *aide-memoire* printed on the grocery pad. Teri scanning the Family Section of the Sunday *Star*. "It says here that our universal fears are dying, disfigurement and madness." "I'll take number three," says Annie. "I stopped being a Catholic when I was twelve," says Philip, beginning a game of reminiscences. "Really! The rest was for mother's sake. I actually stopped believing when I discovered that masturbation was a sin." Their mood is congenial. They have captured time. Sunday stretches before them in an endless pattern of recurrence and recapitulation. Nothing is lost and nothing changes. The muffins are delicious. Philip has two and smokes one of Annie's Matinees. When the telephone rings he allows himself a moment of dulcet anticipation. "Your turn, Father Phil. And if it's family tell them we've gone to Mass."

The cats are chasing their tails in the hallway. The late morning sun floods the living-room. In the kitchen he can hear the sisters talking but he cannot make out their words. On such a Sunday Eugene might call.

The receiver is slippery against his fingertips.

The receiver rests upon its hook. It is black.

Messages.

"That was Rick," he says, picking at the loose skin beside his thumbnail. "He called to say that Chuck Waunch is dead. He was in a motorcycle accident last night somewhere between Wanapitei and Hanmer. He was driving very fast without a helmet." He tears fiercely at the skin, making his thumb bleed. He sucks the blood. "Rick's father is trying to trace his family for the police. No one knows where he came from."

Teri suppresses a nervous giggle. "I'm sorry. I don't mean to laugh. It's the way you said it. 'Chuck Waunch is dead.' It sounds ridiculous and you're wearing your Jesus face." She begins to cry.

"Shut up," says Annie. She taps the muffin tray with a butter knife. Tap, tap, tap.

Red

I have hair like Ethel Kennedy's. I am about her age, too. Around
the compound I wear chinos and T-shirts without a bra. People
say that from ten yards away I look half as old. Up close they
can see the broken veins and alligator skin from too much New
Mexico sun.

Red doesn't like me to wear a bra. "Let 'em hang," he says.
"I like to see 'em swing and bounce." It doesn't matter who hears
as far as he's concerned. "Large and useful, that's what I like.
Don't give me any of those teeny twenty-year-old titties." Red's
from Texas. As Sylvie says, Red's a trip.

I also have long thoroughbred legs and a high ass from playing field hockey at Smith. I married an Amherst boy out of college
when we were both still virgins. He was a tall blond dream from
Missouri who wore specs instead of glasses, played a mean banjo
and walked with a limp from a riding injury. His name was Jack
Titus. He gave me three children: Sylvie, Francine and Pierre. All
three are, to use Sylvie's words, fucked up, a condition for which,
they claim, I am mostly to blame. Sylvie has as much as said,

"If you hadn't left Jack, I'd never have gotten mixed up with Leo." Leo is a pill-popping, glue-sniffing loser who has put her in the hospital twice from car accidents. Franky and Pierre, twenty-six and twenty-four respectively, still haven't managed to leave home. They sit around watching me, trying to make me feel guilty. Red calls them "the yard birds."

When I met Red, I was getting ready to die in Kansas City. This was ten years ago. I had given up the kids to various branches of the family, and I was down to my last $38 and no job. I went to a K-Mart and bought a cheap bikini to die in, then checked into the downtown Holiday Inn and parked myself beside the pool. My plan was to lie there in the sun, buying drinks on a tab until the management asked for money. Then I would suck in my cheeks, assume an air of impregnable Smithy hauteur, stride to the elevator and throw myself out an upper-storey window. It would have worked, too, except on the second day I met Red.

It was about 11 a.m. and I was already smashed. He was wearing lime green Bermuda shorts, a Hawaiian shirt out of a Douanier-Rousseau jungle, and flip-flops. His skin was the colour of boiled lobster; his hair looked as if it had been dipped in red ink. When I first saw him, his face was set in a fierce, creased expression that made me think he was mad at me for something. And when he spoke, he stood so close that the ashes from his cigar fell on my bare stomach.

"You wanna hold my cucumber, honey?" he said, snatching the cigar out of his mouth to take a long pull on his highball glass. I pushed my sunglasses down my nose and examined him over the lenses. He was over six feet tall. His head was in the sun. All I could see was a gut like a basketball jutting from under his shirt. I started to giggle.

"Hey lady, it's pay or play," he said. "In Mexico I've had women fight for what I got. I've had prima donnas like you beg for it. Name your price, sweetheart."

His shirt was streaked with sweat where it hung over his belly. As he spoke, a drop slipped from his nose and fell on my chin. I stuck out my tongue and tasted it. I saw his eyes follow my tongue. I started to laugh and couldn't stop until I got the hiccups. He was grinning; he liked making me laugh.

42

"Name's Red Mulvaney," he said, gesturing with his cigar. "I build shopping centres, drink and whore all the time, and if I keep it up, the doctors say I'll live another five years—tops. Hell, I got a lotta living to do!"

He took another drink and shoved the cigar between his teeth. His eyes were sparkling. They were honest eyes. He was vulgar and crude, but after Jack I'd had enough of nice and evasive. I was ready for vulgar and crude. Hell, I had about five days left and a lot of living to do, too.

"I've only slept with two men in my life," I said, adjusting my straps so he'd stop looking down my chest. "One was my husband, the other was my divorce lawyer. I only did it once with the lawyer because he was a pervert. I'm telling you this so you won't be disappointed."

He dropped down on his haunches so that his face was even with mine. His eyes were leaf green with red flecks, like pimento.

"I've been watching you since you checked in," he said. "I say you're sad and you don't give a shit who you disappoint. I say something's snapped inside and you don't care what anyone thinks. We've got a lot in common. I'll never be disappointed."

Unaccountably, I started to cry. Twenty years with Jack and we had never been this intimate. I felt as if Red had ripped open my chest and left my heart beating in the air. Suddenly I knew how lonely I had been. I wept and wept. People were staring; the waiters looked as if they were afraid I'd clear the pool deck. But Red didn't try to stop me. He let me blow my nose on his shirttail, then ambled off to buy me lunch, my first square meal in a week. Afterward, up in his room, I talked for eight hours straight, then fell over asleep on his bed. He hadn't touched me and the last thing I remember him saying was, "You get some sleep, Flo. You need it. You can hold my cucumber in the morning."

Franky went to law school in Boulder, but she's failed her bar admission exams three years running. Pierre is gay; he works as a waiter at the Gold Bar in Santa Fe. Six months ago, Franky got pulled over for speeding on the interstate and gave the cop a blow-job to let her go. "And I paid for four years of law school," says Red. Though he's not mad. He laughs.

It has been ten good years and he's not dead yet. As far as I know he's never been unfaithful, and he's only hit me once. The worst thing that's happened was when he took Pierre hunting quail in the Jornada one winter and Pierre shot him in the back with a 12-gauge by accident. Even then, Pierre fainted and Red had to carry him back to the truck.

We were married in his room at the Holiday Inn about a week after I discovered sex. Red was right; I didn't care. I tried everything, and everything was just great. Red wired money and plane tickets to each of the kids, but only Sylvie showed up in time. When she came through the door, we were getting dressed for the wedding. Red was in his bathrobe; I had on my bikini bottoms and one of his Hawaiian shirts. She came through the door objecting: "Mother, this isn't like you. Are you out of your ever-loving, fucking mind?" When she saw Red, she started to cry. She sat out the ceremony in the bathroom, sniffling behind her dark glasses and popping downers. By the end of the day she was so stoned we left her in our bed and rented another room down the hall. When we made love it was like hot steel running through my body, and when we slept I held Red's face tight to my breasts to stop the ache.

A week later Red flew us all from K.C. to Roswell, where his company was building a shopping centre. We were living in a mobile home on the site, and the kids were almost comatose. There was nothing for miles around but mesquite, creosote and wandering steers. The three of them sat in front of the TV from noon till dawn, watching the soaps, the weather forecasts, the late night movies and M.A.S.H. repeats, smoking dope they had bought from the Mexican labourers. At night they'd call Jack to tell him what Red had done that day. I understood. Red was hard to love and easy to hate, just the opposite of Jack. "You wouldn't believe it," they'd whisper into the receiver. "We're living in a mall that's not even built yet. It's a forest of I-beams. He took her bowling. *Bowling*, Daddy. And yesterday they were shooting beer cans in the desert. Daddy, you've just got to save us!" It was in Roswell that they began trying to bring Jack and me together. And Jack egged them on, said he wanted to remarry. That was the meanest thing he ever did, making his kids believe in him like that.

Weekends we drove into the mountains to explore the Spanish and Indian villages, hunting up secluded Penitente chapels, buying blankets in Chimayo or pots in San Ildefonso, watching the Pueblo sacred dances as the calendar turned.

One day Red said he had something special to show me and we drove up to Santa Fe, then east along the highway to Pecos. Just outside the town, he pulled off onto a dirt lane that led into a small V-shaped valley with pines climbing up its slopes and a stream running down from the Blood of Christ Mountains. Below us stretched the flood plain of the Pecos River and the ruins of an old Spanish mission like the hulk of a ship at sea. "This is home," he said. "I bought this for you and the kids. I know you all hate that itty-bitty trailer back there. We need something that's just for us."

He meant that—literally. The house we live in, the compound, nobody touched but Red and I. We lived in a tent that summer while building our first adobe room. Sylvie came out to visit; she was with Leo by then. Leo stayed in the car while Sylvie walked up the hill in her dark glasses, sweat pants and Christian Dior sailor shirt. "Mother, I can't believe you're doing this to us," she said. I was mixing mortar; Red was shovelling it into a wheelbarrow and manhandling it up a ramp to the top of our wall. His face was sunburned and peeling. He had a cigar in his mouth. There was a cooler of Dos Equis beside the mortarbox. I don't think we had seen another human being for a week.

"Pierre is suicidal, Franky is fucking a Mexican chili cook named Felipe, and every man I go out with is a jerk," said Sylvie. "And all you do is play in the mud with this over-sexed, macho, crypto-fascist pig." She took off her sunglasses and said, almost in a whisper, "Jack is in the hospital again. I think you should go and see him."

As the years passed we added to the house: five rooms, a solarium, a sauna and a stable. When things got comfortable enough, the kids moved back. I discovered a talent for potting; Red helped me build a studio and kiln. For a whole year we spent every spare moment wandering across the state, learning everything we could from the Indians about the old ways of turning and firing and applying glaze. I made friends with the museum administrators in Sante Fe. One day I woke up and found I was a local expert who could sell pots, sometimes for as much as a thousand dollars. Red was proud, but he never said a word.

Instead, he hit me. This happened about a year ago. He had flown in that morning from a construction site in Silver City. He came barging into the studio about mid-afternoon after stopping at a couple of bars to find the mood, gruff as usual, drunk as per same, saying nothing, just wanting to see me. I was finishing a storage pot in the Mimbres style, large as a bushel basket. It had taken me two months from scratch. Red hefted it in his muscular hands; he likes to fondle the things I make almost as much as he likes to fondle the maker. Somehow he lost his grip and the pot slipped, first to the work table, then to the floor where it broke. I went down on my knees without a word, and when I looked up, he was gone. I wanted to run after him then, but I held back. I knew he hated pity and condescension.

At dinner he made up a fight over the posole. When I argued back, he slapped me good and hard across the face. Franky and Pierre were goggle-eyed, straining their necks like turtles on the other side of the table. I was crying and they were staring and Red took a bottle from the cabinet with him down to the creek. I wanted to explain how badly Red felt that he had broken my pot. I wanted to tell them how I would hug him in bed that night even when he tried to turn away. How I would hug him till he knew he was forgiven. But I knew they wouldn't understand. For some reason they are afraid of life and take it out on me.

Red never said he loved me; nor I him. At the Holiday Inn in Kansas City we had struck a deal. I told him I had three children I wanted to keep with me and support through college. I was being blunt; I was also holding his cucumber. "I love children," he said. I have to say he didn't bat an eye. But then, unlike Jack, who hyperventilated and had to breathe into a paper bag every time anyone so much as mentioned getting a job, Red never had trouble with money. He spent it as fast as he made it, but he was always making it.

For his part, Red admitted it wasn't quite true what he had said about all the drinking and whoring. Until a year and a half before we met, he had been married to a Mexican woman called Patrice, an abstract expressionist painter in the style of Ruffino Tamayo, who had died of a stroke. They had run into each other in Upper Volta one year while he was building the sluice gates on a power dam for the government; Patrice was backpacking, studying African primitives. When she failed to conceive, she "went Catholic" instead of going to see a doctor, according to Red. She even got him to go to Mass, praying for a child that never came. "She was a difficult woman," he said, shaking his head. "But I can't forget her. Take me, and you'll just have to put up with her like a ghost in a house." I cried all the time he was telling me the story. I had never met a man so romantic. Sometimes I think I had just never met a man.

Jack was just the opposite. Jack lied every time he opened his mouth. He lied when he said "good morning" or "how are you?" It wasn't that he was trying to be cruel; he would always explain his prevarication by saying he only wanted to make me happy. I didn't know until the second year of our marriage that he was an alcoholic. I didn't know until he went into the hospital with acute alcohol poisoning and the doctor told me himself. "But Jack doesn't drink," I said, all innocence and wounded pride. "Lady, when your husband came in here, he had more bourbon than blood in his veins."

Jack's mother never gave me any help. She said the same thing every time it happened: "He is such a sensitive boy. He always gets like this when he's tired and drinks too much coffee. I think he's allergic to coffee." I went a whole year saying, "Jack, maybe you should lay off the coffee this morning." Jack just looked at me as if I were a loon.

If Jack was allergic to anything, it was to work. First he wanted to be a writer. So I bought him a typewriter with money left over from the wedding. When he decided to be a drummer in a band, I became suspicious. We moved to Florida and had Sylvie. Jack panicked; he was in the hospital seeing rats before I took the

47

baby home. He was "on the wagon" when Franky was born. Every morning he went straight to the kitchen for a large glass of fresh-squeezed orange juice—which was mostly vodka. He got a job in a bank owned by some relative, stole $8,000 in American Express travelers' cheques, and left a trail of bad paper that led the police to the Bide-A-Wee Motel in Lincoln, Nebraska, where he was living with a college girl. He had told her he was a writer. For a couple of years after Pierre was born, Jack seemed to pull himself together. He picked his banjo, read books about Jesse James, and stopped robbing the kids' piggy banks. He went back to being the charming, urbane, affectionate boy I'd met at the Amherst mixer. That was about as close as he ever got to being a responsible father.

My family was floating loans to support us. I had a part-time job as a representative for a tea company. I drove around to sports events, fairs and public meetings in a van that opened up at the back to serve free samples. My boss liked to tell me that if Smith had taught me anything it had taught me how to pour tea. Jack stayed with the kids; he was a kid himself. He always had a grin on his face when I came through the door, always had a wisecrack or a funny story and a pair of idle hands to help with the groceries.

We were living in K.C. then, though his parents had ceased to give us any money. And it was while I was working on the tea wagon and Jack was being so nice that he was also having an affair with our dentist's wife, who met him mornings at the Muehlebach Hotel. He panicked when I caught on. I wasn't mad. I was willing to let things go. But Jack ran off with a go-go dancer he was convinced needed protection from the mob. She called me from Fargo. He'd told her he was a drummer in a band and that he limped because he'd been shot robbing a bank. That was when I left him.

Sylvie and I have had many heart-to-hearts about this. She believes she speaks for the family. And maybe she does. Sylvie says she is caught between two worlds and doesn't know where to turn. She wants to be an artist, and Red pays for her to study printmaking with Lazansky in Iowa. But she claims she can't commit herself as deeply as she must because of the divorce.

She can't build a life on shifting sands, she says. Everything vanishes. No one can be trusted. She is afraid of failure because she thinks I failed.

Once in a while, when she has been staying with Red and me for a few weeks and has settled down, she gets as far as saying, "But Daddy was always nice to us. He couldn't have been that bad, could he?" I never say anything, nor does Red. This was something I decided early on, this silence, though I knew Jack would be telling his side of the story to anybody who would listen until the day he died.

Sometimes, when Sylvie has been especially hard on me, Red cannot restrain himself. "You kids sure have been dealt a bad hand," he'll say. "You got the best mother in the world, all the money you could ever want, a home you can come to in God's own country—shit, you got every reason to take a gun off that wall there and put yourselves out of your misery." He'll poke the fire, muttering to himself for a while, then add: "Shells are in the top right-hand drawer."

They're like their father; they've decided to be unhappy.

One night Red and I are alone, lying naked in front of the fireplace in our bedroom, with a tripod of piñon logs spitting and throwing our shadows on the whitewashed walls that surround us. We are listening to Lotta Lenya singing songs from the *Three Penny Opera*, from an old album of Red's. He's got an original 1930s recording made in Berlin and a 1950s version cut during a performance at the Théâtre de Lys in New York. Patrice had taken him to see the show on their honeymoon, and the album has a skip where they knocked a candle on it while making love. Somehow I never feel jealous of Patrice. I can tell Red loved her so much that my jealousy would be next to blasphemy.

Around us are the trophies of our ten-year marriage: Kachina dolls, the drawings I copied from potsherds, framed and mounted on the walls we built with our own hands. Next to the chimney hangs Patrice's last painting, a crimson figure with his arms out-flung, shining like the sun. There are also photographs of the children and me that Red took. The kids are shy and crabby in front of the lens, but we crowd together as if seeking that family feeling we all miss.

We are lying together when the telephone rings. It's Sylvie, sounding desperate. Leo's been arrested in Stone City, Iowa, wasted on coke, after sideswiping five parked cars outside an all-night roadhouse. She loves him, she feels sorry for him, but she wants to leave him. Maybe she will kill herself. She has decided she will never be able to lead a normal life unless she is somehow sure Jack and I were never meant for each other. Her voice, thin and weary at the other end of the line, is like a knife in my ribs. My firstborn is twenty-eight, confused, and trapped in events that took place over a decade ago. In a moment of weakness, I tell her I'll do anything to make her happy, though I know what's to come. She wants me to meet Jack, whom I have not laid eyes on since the divorce. I know this is her fantasy quest, her dream reunion. She wants the clock turned back.

I have overheard the three of them, Sylvie, Franky and Pierre, discussing this when they think I am out of the house. They imagine us appearing to each other out of the gloom in a darkened bar. They see our eyes meet with a look of startled recognition, then we approach each other timidly, warily, like wild animals. Suddenly our love is rekindled: we talk in the old bantering way they remember; we sip our drinks; we share one chaste kiss and part, forever. Even in their ideal visions, the kids cannot get Jack out of a bar or force us to remarry. But they think they could live with the divorce if I would admit it was a mistake.

According to Sylvie, Jack is living in Aspen now, where he runs a service station with a woman named Marge. She says he is willing to come down if I agree to see him. Her voice is breaking; I know she may never speak to me again if I don't say yes. I tip-toe back to the fireplace to tell Red the arrangements. Jack will take a room at La Posada for the weekend at the kids' (meaning Red's) expense. I am to rendezvous with him in the courtyard Saturday afternoon. I tell Red we are just going to talk for my children's benefit, but as I say the words I am conscious of my own ambiguity. Sylvie has planted the phrase "what if" in my head, though I am only doing it for her sake. Red has never said "what if" in his life. That is why it's so easy for me to bear his love for the dead Patrice. He mourns, but he never regrets. And now he says nothing. Just grunts. Which is Texan for "Do whatever you like."

Red cannot speak of things that are close to his heart, and because of that people like Sylvie often think he doesn't have one. She also thinks that the way he has of remembering Patrice is a kind of infidelity. She does not want complexity and refuses to see that Red is an ugly, gentle man who grew up in a place where gentleness was hidden out of necessity. When Red starts playing his albums, Sylvie will recall that Jack used to own every record Bob Dylan ever made. But she has never felt Red's body stiffen with pain and longing when Lotta begins to sing *The Black Ship*. She will never know.

On Saturday Red drops me at the plaza in front of the Palace of Governors and heads for his dermatologist. Once a year he has the skin cancers removed from his face. With his complexion, he was never meant to live in the south, but, like me, he loves the sun. Red's been good about this get-together with Jack. He hasn't said a word, treating it like another lunch with one of my museum pals. As far as I can tell, he doesn't have a jealous bone in his body. He says he'll pick me up in a couple of hours.

I stroll lazily up San Francisco toward Archbishop Lamy's Gothic revival cathedral. I stop to watch a juggler, a child on roller skates, a Pueblo woman selling turquoise. I idle along because I do not know where I am going. I know La Posada, of course, but I do not know where I am going in my mind. I recall Jack during our courtship, his corny, winning ways, his slightly Edwardian air, the nights he serenaded me, strumming his banjo and singing Missouri ballads beneath my bedroom window. Whenever I dated another boy, Jack tailed us in his battered Hudson. He wrote love letters every day, left messages for me in classrooms, at the dry cleaners, at the cafe where I went evenings, at the residence desk. "Save a sigh for a drowning man," he wrote, seeing himself always as the underdog. When it came time for me to make a decision, Jack had simply out-lasted his competition.

Stepping through the adobe arch, I find him watching the street with an anxious expression that alters suddenly into that pleased, boyish grin I remember so well. Only now I see that one of his front teeth has been capped and the enamel is discoloured. He's wearing jeans, a Levi's workshirt and moccasins. His hair still falls over his forehead, but his eyes are lined, darker. Still slim and tall, he is no longer ageless, though aging gracefully. I am aware, as I always was before, that we are a striking couple. He clutches a red rose, long-stemmed, in his hand, which looks silly, and when he passes it to me, I feel silly. All of a sudden I see what I never noticed before, that Jack does everything a beat off, like an actor missing his cue; that his gestures and protestations are always slightly marred, hypocritical, sheepish, embarrassing. But he always means well, I say to myself. The old apologetic refrain.

As he escorts me through the vestibule past the desk clerk and into the bar, I note that his collar and cuffs are comfortably worn, that his jeans bag a little in the ass. Actually he's slimmer than I recall, too thin. He waits for me to decide where we will sit, a barstool or an armchair by the unused fireplace. I choose the deep, threadbare comfort of a sofa by the window, and catch Jack winking at the bartender, a man with whom I am sure he has been holding intimate colloquy since long before my arrival. I place the rose on the floor with my bag, thankful to be able to get it out of sight. Jack orders a bourbon on the rocks, a double, and a Mexican beer for me. His hand shakes as he reaches for the glass. Above the wrist, his arm is pale. Crossing his legs, he leans back, languid and graceful, yet in a way exhausted. He has had a hard life keeping up with himself.

So far we have spoken very little beyond the usual pleasantries. I realize that I want Jack to be bowled over by me. In spite of myself, I have spent a good two hours getting ready for this, and I am dressed to kill. That's why I am suddenly angry, angry with myself. The whole modus operandi of our marriage was me trying to make an impression on Jack, trying to make him see what his drinking did to us, trying to make him happy to keep him from drinking, just trying to make him notice. But after being hopelessly infatuated with me for six months leading up to the wedding, his ego has remained impervious to mortal wiles ever since. Worst of all, I liked him being infatuated. It appealed to my lowest instincts, but I liked it. So wanting him to be bowled over now is a kind of revenge I have been planning; but as usual, Jack is unreachable.

"How's Red?" he asks slyly. His smile is not quite a smirk.

"How's Marge?" I ask back. I know he wants to put me on the defensive, and I don't care so long as we don't discuss Red. Red saved me from dying because of this man. After a decade, Red is still sacred. I will not have him spoken of in ways that diminish him.

"Marge is a good friend," he says, laughing. Jack will run anybody down behind his back. "She's good-hearted."

Interpreting what Sylvie has told me, I gather that Marge is an overweight, depressed woman who also drinks too much but manages to keep food on the table by pumping gas twelve hours a day when she's sober. I hope she gives him a sharp knee in the balls if he ever calls her "good-hearted" within ear-shot.

Aware that his charm is ineffective, Jack makes an effort to be frank and affectionate. This is his second line of defense; after the rifle pits and forward trenches have fallen, he becomes frank and affectionate.

"Well, it's good to see you. It was worth the trip. The kids have been working their darned little butts off to get us together," he says. He rattles on about what good kids they are. Jesus, I don't like this man. I wasted twenty years on him, and it only makes me mad to think I am washing yet another afternoon of my life down the same drain.

"Our kids are just like you," I say. "They haven't come to grips with the difference between the way the world works and their daydreams. For the time being, they're blaming this disparity on our divorce. It's not pleasant to watch. But I keep telling myself I had to stagger through a bad marriage into middle-age before I grew up."

I order another beer because I see that I am talking too much. That's always a bad thing to do with Jack. He's the white hunter of the conversational jungle; he sets traps. Red wouldn't have put up with this for thirty seconds. Red would have taken advantage of one of Jack's nerve-racking silences to walk out of the bar and into another one farther down the street.

"We all have to learn to accept ourselves, the good and the

bad," says Jack, who accepts himself by signalling for a triple.

"I feel out-manoeuvred," I say, and he smiles. "Sylvie's been after me for ages to give you another chance. Now I see that talking is never going to decide anything."

"It's just nice to be together again," he asserts blandly, ignoring what I have just said. "It's been a long time."

I am practically blind with anger now. I know I am over-reacting; I haven't resolved all my self-hatred and disgust for the years I spent hoping Jack would miraculously reform, thinking somehow that I could perform the functions of mother, wife and redeeming angel all at once. "Sylvie means well," I catch myself thinking. And then, out of the corner of my eye, I see Red in the doorway, a bandage patched over the bridge of his nose, his eyes hunting for me. He's wearing pale blue shorts, an amazing ruby-coloured V-neck sweater and sneakers with the toes cut out. In the normal run of events, Red can carry off this costume up to and including formal dinner parties. But today he suddenly looks out of place, frail and a little afraid.

I check my watch; he's early. He catches my eye, nods, then heads over to the bar, out of sight. Jack has been staring wistfully out the window and hasn't noticed. I'm not sure he would even recognize Red. But it's a mess anyway because the bartender knows us by name and he'll guess that something funny is going on. It's not like Red to put himself in that kind of position. In my mind there is a stampede of images: the rose, the bandage on Red's face, my divorce lawyer prancing around in lace undies, Sylvie crying in her chair, Franky and Pierre huddled in silent conspiracy.

I know Red likes people to be decisive. I retrieve Jack's rose and hand it back to him, bloom first, like a sword. Then I grab my bag and say, "Would you excuse me, please?" I can see he's puzzled. I am probably going to the bathroom, he thinks. But why give him the rose?

I am slipping up to the bar before he can wipe that smirk off his face and utter a word. I am nudging Red's elbow, saying softly, "Buy me a drink, sweetheart." Then he turns to me and gives me a shock. A drop of blood has seeped through the gauze on his nose, tiny pinheads of sweat are running together over his brow, and there are tears sliding down his cheeks.

I take his hand and give it a squeeze.

"I love you, Flo," he says. "If you leave me, I'll blow my brains out."

That's Red, I think. When you need him, he's there. He lets you know where you stand. He takes your breath away.

"I love you, Red," I say in a strong voice. "One day we'll die together— it's the only way." And having said this, I am suddenly sure that we will live forever.

The Irredeemable

There were four of them, counting the dog; four of God's creatures living in the grey clapboard house far down what used to be called the Blue Line in Charles County near Kingston. They were Darryl Foxman, his wife Letty, the boy Walt and the old dog Henry.

Darryl was the son of Leyland Foxman, a direct descendant of a Major Leyland Foxman who had come to Canada with his family from New Jersey after the Revolution. The major had surrendered with Burgoyne, but later slipped away to New Orleans, broke his parole and fought on after the war was lost. A Foxman fell at Queenston Heights; the blood of reaction thins slowly in the veins of country men.

Faded sepia photographs of later generations of Foxmans showed big-headed stern-faced men and women with harsh humourless features that might have been hewn from the earth itself with pick and spade, hawk-eyes glowing with fanaticism, and horny angular hands. Yet, like many proud families, the Foxmans carried a private taint in their bitter fanatical blood. The generations grew weaker and uglier and scarcer. Hereditary disease and barrenness drew the clan's strength like the old-time quack bleeders. Darryl's twin brothers died at birth. A sister was childless. Darryl Foxman himself was once reputed to be the ugliest man in the county, with his stubby fireplug body, cheeks like ploughshares, nose like an axe handle and forehead like the blade of a shovel.

Letty was the daughter of a sickly Methodist preacher sent by the diocese to open the old church in Ockenden about the time the young men were returning from the war with Hitler. She was the sourest and eldest of four girls. And when her father died shortly thereafter, moving to that better living beyond, she took a grim pride in rearing the other three and marrying them off before beginning to scout around on her own behalf. If the truth were told, the sisters took to marriage with an almost unseemly haste, seeing it not so much as the acquisition of a good, or even an indifferent, man, as an escape from Letty's rough tenderness. When she finally did start to hunt for a husband of her own, all she could come up with was a lonesome gargoyle, fit for the rainspouts of a gothic cathedral, named Darryl Foxman.

Over the years their union was blessed, or cursed, once; and after that Darryl was no more thought of as the ugliest man in the county. Young Walt had the clearest, finest, meekest soul; he had intelligence and curiosity, integrity, kindness and sensitivity. But he was born an unnatural, unhealthy, ghostly shade of white. It was clear God had meant him for some other world, or only half made him for this. He was repulsive as the bloated body of a drowned man, fat with rolls of doughy chemical fat, and nearly blind so that he had to wear glasses with thick lenses like the sealers farm women use to close jam jars. And as he grew up he came to speak with a gasping stutter so that people thought he was dim as well as ugly.

Thus to the Foxman ugliness and bitterness and Letty's sourness was added young Walt's goodness, which only made things worse. The house remained silent and lonely. And beneath the veil of silence the linked emotions of the three people twisted and knotted like a snake half-severed with an axe. To keep himself sane, Walt would walk alone in the woods with his dog, never telling anyone of his misery which was worst when he saw himself in a mirror and was frightened at his own hideousness.

Old Henry, the dog, a mutt with a predominance of Border Collie, a remnant of the time when Scottish immigrants tried to range sheep in the county, entered the picture soon after Walt was born. Both parents realized early on that natural affection was not going to well forth from their bone-dry disappointed hearts, and, not having the courage to make a second child, they decided a dog would have to serve as a stand-in for normal human warmth and love. Darryl chose the runt from a neighbour's litter saying "It ain't no use wasting more'n a runt on a runt." But it did serve.

It was as if Henry understood and sympathized with his master's affliction for he never tolerated strangers and would snarl and raise his back-hairs when anyone new came near the boy. With Letty and Darryl he was dignified and aloof. He was a good watch-dog, killed groundhogs and bit an Indian. Not that that endeared him any. As the years limped by in sadness, the dog perversely began to resemble the boy. He grew obese and grey; his eyes turned pink and he began to go blind and deaf. His breath was foul and he farted continuously the king of all dog farts, full of rat droppings and rotting fat from ancient barnyard slaughterings.

He took to lying all day on the bottom step of the front porch, a self-willed invitation to destruction. A person would gauge his footfall to miss old Henry and a leg or a tail would flop out at the last instant to stand victim. And the dog would rise in a flurry of doggy screams, snapping at the errant foot, drawing curses and perhaps a bag of groceries on his innocent head.

How sour Letty came to hate that dog. In this hierarchy of martyrs, Henry was low man. He drew the distilled acid of bitterness that dripped down through all the ugliness and resentment and frustration, corroding the steely fanaticism and stubbornness of the elder Foxman, falling on the petrified spirit of Letty until she was no more than a pillar of bitter salt, a soul-stalactite in the cave of time, and thence to Henry.

So it inevitably happened that Letty decided the dog should die, should become a scapegoat, a replacement for the death of a child, the death of love. And she suggested this, not realizing that in a way Henry was a keystone in their crazy emotional arch, the last tattered remnant of feeling, the last remote misshapen piece of connective tissue without which they were little more than substantial molecules whirling in some dark soulless night.

"That there dog ought to be put down," she croaked one evening in a barely audible nasal twang.

They were all four sitting in the kitchen. Letty and Walt were candling eggs for delivery the next day; Darryl was musing on a half-seen mezzotint of some cruel piratical ancestor across the room. The dog was making his presence known by a series of flaps and hisses, like a kettle with a loose lid, the smell often pervading the kitchen like a lethal miasma, a strong reminder of mortality, a humble aroma. At the sound of Letty's voice, the dog flopped his tail on the faded linoleum floor, the bony joints sounding like dice thrown in a back alley, stretched happily and emitted an even louder, more rancid series of farts.

"Oh," she moaned. "That disgusting animal!"

"H-h-h-he can't h-h-he-ulp it, Ma," stuttered Walt, his head bobbing like a sandpiper in the effort of speaking. "H-h-h-he don't mean n-n-n-no h-a-rum."

Letty winced. As time wore on, she had come to tolerate common sense less and less. She confused it with male pigheadedness, as more and more her whims took on the substance of reality. The world for Letty was what she saw on a screen in front of her when the light came from the back of her soul where sourness and bitterness burned like swamp gas throwing up the shadows of her dreams as truth. She hated it even worse when reason and common sense came on the crippled lips of her monstrous son.

"He stinks and he isn't healthy," she squeaked. "And you don't know anything about it. It'd be a mercy to put him out of his misery. Can't be happy living in pain like that."

Walt could hear the parlour clock ticking off the seconds like beaten pots, the click and scrape of the eggs, the dog's flapping and hissing. He looked down at Henry who was manifestly content in the world and assayed another clap of his thin tail as if to prove the point.

The colour rose from somewhere in Walt's chest, up past his

half-dozen chalk-like trembling chins and his balloon cheeks to the roots of his sparse white hair. The heat from his flesh misted his glasses.

"H-h-h-he ain't worse'n any old dog, M-m-m-ma. He's got a good couple of years s-s-s-sittin' in the sun y-y-y-ye-ut." His voice rose and fell unnaturally. "Don't get ek-ek-ek-ek-hecksited, Ma."

The elder Foxman, in his peculiarly phlegmatic way, stirred uneasily in his chair, then rose, nudging the dog roughly with the paint-specked cracked leather toe of his work-boot. He opened the back door to the woodshed and hustled the dog outside. Henry's expression of dignified contentment turned to terror and remorse. He looked over his shoulder as he stumbled through the door, his rheumy eyes wondering what he had done to deserve this awful ostracism. He stood outside the door whining thinly through worn-down teeth and then composed himself to sleep on an old tarpaulin.

"Leave that dog out there," Darryl Foxman said to everyone in general in a gruff, rasping voice. Then to Letty: "Leave that dog alone!"

The order was full of menace, but only apparently so, for the husband knew his wife and knew that no threat had the slightest effect. The challenge to battle had been issued, that was all. The ugly man sat in his chair and recommenced contemplating his glorious ancestors, preferring that oblivion to trying to curb Letty's agile will. She had that almost obscene tenaciousness of womankind, the ability to lose all sense of perspective, bury dignity and reason, in pursuit of a goal. It was wearying to live with her.

The woman let out a cold severe sigh like a cat spitting and mechanically went on with her work. It was difficult to say what she wanted out of life, she was that sour on it. Her ambition found satisfaction in little victories which she hoarded like a miser. A man might dream of owning land or starting a business or going to war or writing a book, but not Letty. The Lord was with her most when she got back the wrong change at the supermarket and found she'd made money. Or when she convinced Walt to give up going to school dances because he might be ridiculed. Or when, after a campaign of years, she finally got Darryl to let her take over the egg business on her own. It was this ability to consolidate small gains that made her so formidable an opponent. There was little deception, only a low unwearying cunning. She was implacable like a snake after a mouse.

And so it was only mildly surprising when, after a truce of a couple of days, the man and the youth returned from work one noon to find that Letty had contrived to trip over Henry and smash the morning's eggs on the altar of the front porch. She was sitting like some Old Testament prophet in a rocking chair beside the screen door, a long-handled broom across her lap, her lips clenched like the edge of a razor blade. Drying yolks and broken shells lay strewn at her feet. Henry cowered in the crawlspace beneath the steps just out of reach. And, as Darryl and Walt approached, congruent grotesques, he flopped his balding tail against a porch beam in welcome.

"That dog of yours just cost us eight dollars in eggs and darn near broke my leg," croaked Letty. "That dog is past supporting. He ought to be dead. And I'll kill him myself if I catch him."

Like some comic vaudeville team, the two males looked at the woman, then at Henry's hiding place, then at each other, and then at the woman again. It was obvious to them that whatever the dog's physical infirmities were, he was still in full possession of his mental faculties and would happily stay under the porch forever in order to avoid Letty. The animal had a streak of furtive sagacity that belied all her attempts to impute to him a sort of canine world-weariness. In fact, from the moment Letty had lain down the gauntlet, so to speak, the dog had perversely set out upon an Indian summer life that infused his moribund body with a puppy's frantically cheerful enthusiasm. The day before he'd gotten so excited at seeing Darryl come out to milk the cows he'd peed on his leg, a dark smelly old-dog pee to be sure, but it was the thought that counted.

Assured of an audience, however unsympathetic or indifferent, Letty abandoned the rocking chair and scrambled down the steps, her eyes bulging with spleen. She knelt on the bottom plank and squinted into the dark cavity. At the same time, her faded print dress hiked up over her sunken flanks revealing a pale stretch of slack-veined leg between rolled-up stockings on jar-ring garters and a pair of holey cotton underpants.

"I'll poke his darn eyes out," she puffed hoarsely.

Henry retreated into the crawlspace as she plunged the broom handle towards him. Darryl gazed at Letty's flanks through tight rimless glasses as though he were an amateur botanist examining a new weed. Walt coloured and looked at his mother's head.

She stabbed away like a demonic whaler until her arms began to tire. One final lunge brought the broom close by Henry's ear, so close the dog felt obliged to curl his lips and snarl briefly as a modest expression of his dissatisfaction with fate.

Letty flung herself back from the steps exclaiming. "What'd I tell you? The dog's gone mad with age. D'you see the way he snapped at me? What are you going to do about it, Darryl? You going to stand there like a sick cow or are you going to put that dog down?"

It was all such a fabrication that the male Foxmans could do little more than smile sheepishly and try to brush the egg shell and chicken dirt off Letty's knees and dress. Had they had a bit more feminine guile in their poor straightforward masculine heads they would have realized that an untruth with a kernel of evidence to back it up will become gospel in the hands of a determined woman. They did not see that what appeared so ridiculous to them in context would three days hence bear the ring of authenticity in the presence of neighbours.

Without thinking of these consequences, Walt and Darryl succeeded in calming Letty down and dragging her into the house to take a cup of tea. Later in the day, Walt brought some scraps for Henry on a plate which he pushed under the steps. And the next day Letty nailed up a sign at the entrance to the farm laneway. It said: BEWARE OF VICIOUS DOG.

Having established that Henry was unsanitary, unhappy, ill, dangerous, ugly and old, Letty now appeared to ease up in her campaign for execution. Walt began to hope that his dog might somehow come to live out his naturally allotted span. The woman even took steps to befriend the animal. She started taking him scraps in the morning after the men had gone to the fields. She coaxed him out from under the porch where he now took refuge from dawn until the time Walt and Darryl returned from work. He still didn't go far from his retreat, but he nevertheless felt safe enough to sidle out into the sunlight to sleep fitfully under a cloud of buzzing flies.

This temporary hiatus ended abruptly about a week later when a violent squealing of angry tractor brakes, an inarticulate outburst of male blasphemy, the crunch and crack of machine on wood and Henry's joyful yelping heralded a fresh outbreak of hostilities.

Somehow, and no one ever admitted absolute knowledge of how, the dog's food dish had gotten itself placed in the middle of the lane in front of the drive-shed where the sun was hot and the ground was warm and flat and hospitable. Darryl had finished discing in the low field by the woods and had come driving back quickly in third gear to put the tractor away. He turned the corner round the end of the shed to find Henry lying sacrifically dormant in the path of the machine. Darryl slammed on the brakes and swerved. Henry awoke and began to bark enthusiastically from a recumbent position. And the tractor hurtled by into the shed wall.

"Dish? What dish?" inquired Letty equably when confronted over the kitchen table by her husband a few minutes later. "I don't know anything about the dog's dish. I can't be expected to keep my eye on that creature as if he were a child. He's supposed to have enough sense to keep himself alive."

She pressed her lips together like a piece of string and the tiny ends slipped slightly above the horizontal in a shape faintly reminiscent of a smile.

"Who put the goddamned dish in the driveway? That's all I want to know," shouted Darryl. "That fool has just cost us $500 for a new front axle and a shed door. And that fool is goin' to pay every cent of it outta her egg money."

"Now just a darn minute, Darryl," shouted Letty, easing her temper into gear. "Don't raise your voice at me when it was that dog that got in your way. I'm not paying you a cent. What you do is your business. If you're going to insist on making a fool of yourself over that dog, I can't help it. If you think that dog is worth more than a tractor axle, you go ahead. Break a new one in over his head. But one of us has got to stay sane around here to take care of that helpless boy."

The last was said just as Walt came in the door to see what all the excitement was about. Letty's words made him colour and steam his glasses. He began to pick nervously at some sunburn scabs on his white neck, making himself look like a slab of raw meat. Both parents were ashamed that he had overheard the remark. It made them angrier with each other.

"I ain't killin' no dog to please you, woman. I ain't killin' no dog. And what's more I reckon I'll sell your chickens to pay for my tractor."

"You touch my chickens and I'll put the law on you. It's the dog that did it, not my hens. You haven't got any sense."

"Woman, you are the most stubborn . . ."

"Darryl, it's the dog or me. Take your choice. And if you pick that dog, there won't be any place hot enough for you to go when you're dead, and my daddy'll see to it."

"Go hang the dog, Letty. We ain't talkin' about the dog. I don't care about the dog. My axle's busted and you done it . . ."

Darryl's voice trailed off in impotent rage. Blood vessels were popping in his face like strings of Chinese firecrackers. The air seemed to vibrate like a gun battery at war. All the ugliness and hatred and unhappiness of the household shot like spouts of flame from eye to eye.

Walt felt tears trickling down his jowls, stinging the raw skin, burning the pale flesh. His mother began to cackle in triumph, laughing louder and louder until Darryl's look of anger melted into fear.

The next day Letty had her way. Early in the morning she drove the battered Chevy pick-up into Ockenden and hired the drugstore owner's son, Lyle Farnham, to come out with his .22 that afternoon and put poor vicious old sick Henry out of his misery. For his trouble, Lyle Farnham was promised a dollar out of the egg money Letty kept cached in a tin box in the woodshed.

At lunch she made the announcement just as Walt and Darryl sat down to eat. Walt got up right away and went out to look at his dog. Darryl chewed his food slowly and methodically and silently, his eyes sunk back in his head looking at the dirty mezzotint on the wall. There seemed to him no use in fighting fate any longer. The dog was old and who could say if it might not be better to put him away? If it would bring peace. And yet with all the ugliness, death itself still seemed incomparably worse.

After the meal, he went out and found Walt who was red and raw and steamed up and led him out to the fields to haul some stones. It was Darryl's all-purpose remedy. Whenever he needed to work off anger or spleen or misery, he went out and hauled stones. Sometimes he did haul stones from the fields to the hedgerow by the woods, sometimes he talked to himself, and sometimes he just lay in the grass and thought. This time he decided they really needed to haul stones, anything to pass the time and keep the mind still.

They pulled the stoneboat, a low flat sled on rudimentary plank runners, by hand since the tractor was being repaired. The sun was up and it was hot. They started collecting stones turned up in the spring ploughing, piling them in a pyramid on the boat. Time passed slowly. Sweat dripped off them like holy water. They worked in silence except for the tapping of the stones falling on one another and the harsh rasping of their breath.

Presently the stillness was broken by the popping report of a .22. It echoed off the farm buildings and drifted out to them like a salute. It was over, they knew, yet they would not go back, not till evening.

Walt gasped and heaved his stone down on the pile. That was all. The youth and his father grabbed the leather drawing harness and began to pull the too-heavy load like slaves in Egypt. The harness cut into salty sunburns and the pain was like a benediction that blackened the sun and made the world invisible.

They had just got the stoneboat moving on the white alien soil when the second hollow pop broke on them like an electric shock.

"Hot damn!" hissed Darryl, looking towards the buildings in disbelief.

"Wh-wh-wh-wha-ut is it, Pa?" asked Walt, tears coming as he squinted through his clouded glasses.

"Hot damn! Shit!"

Walt slumped to the stones, moaning over and over, "Oh no. Oh no."

Darryl stood with one hand on his hip, the other scratching the line where his painter's cap dug into the flesh of his forehead. It seemed to him that the beating of their hearts somehow signalled the hot centre of eternity. As he watched, oracular flights of swallows stroked and smoothed the air with frenetic urgency.

A third pop.

The fat fireplug body of Darryl Foxman sprouted legs beneath his coveralls and started to run flat out towards the sound. His little leather-clad feet seemed hardly to touch the ground, leaving only tiny puffs of dust to show where he had been.

Walt was a little slower, struck numb perhaps by the contrast between the world's insane cruelty and the imperturbable serenity of the summer sky. But then he too was up and running, and was even gaining on his father when the two rounded the drive-shed corner and entered the farmyard opposite the house.

Lyle Farnham, pale under his tan, smooth-cheeked, clad in T-shirt, jeans and sneakers, was peering under the porch. He was trembling and his arm-pits were soaked with sweat. He hadn't heard the other two approach and was raising his gun to fire a fourth shot.

Darryl barely slackened his relentless charge. He lengthened his stride over the last three steps and punted Lyle football-style in the bone socket beneath the buttocks. Lyle slammed into the paint-flecked porch railing like a piece of plaster statuary.

"Yow," he yelled. His gun clattered to the stony ground beside him. "Stop, Mr. Foxman. Please stop. I didn't mean no harm. I couldn't get a clear shot at him."

"Get off of this farm," rasped Darryl breathlessly. He picked up the .22. "Get off of this farm before I kill you myself."

"Please, Mr. Foxman," pleaded Lyle, terrified by the two grotesque freaks standing above him. He crawled backwards on his hands in the chicken dirt. "I didn't mean no harm. She paid me to do it. He kept movin' in there. I would have finished him next time."

"Git," roared Darryl in a long drawn-out monosyllable that seemed to shake the buildings.

Lyle turned on his stomach and sprinted like a racer heading for the gate.

"Get back, son," Darryl said quietly. "Hold this." He handed Walt the gun.

He lay in the dirt on his stomach by the worn grass where Henry used to wriggle under the boards into the crawlspace. He squeezed his head and an arm and shoulder into the hole, puffing and wheezing with the effort. From inside came a low-pitched whining growl, the dog's pain and hatred issuing in a blind mad antipathy for all living things.

"Come on, fella. It's old Darryl come to fetch you home."

Walt could hear his father's soft crooning voice coaxing the wounded dog out.

"Come on, Henry, it's okay now."

The growling subsided and was replaced by loud squeaks of pain. Darryl started worming his way out of the hole. His head appeared, then his arm, and finally a hand holding the scruff of Henry's neck.

Lyle had shot the dog three times. One bullet had grazed the top of his head and gone into the shoulder leaving a furrow of matted hair, fat and blood. One had hit him in the mouth, cracking his lower jaw. A third had entered his body somewhere near the haunches.

The ugly old dog lay dying in the dirt, breathing in great barrelling gasps, blood dyeing the white sepulchral earth black. He seemed smaller than usual, nothing but a mangy bag of skin and bones. His tired eyes did not look at the two men any more. They gazed unblinking into the distance, somewhere beyond all the outrage and suffering.

"Son, don't you ever say anything to me about what I'm goin' to do."

"No, Pa."

"Give me that gun."

Walt handed his father the .22. Darryl cocked it, placed the muzzle behind Henry's ear and shot him cleanly. The breathing stopped at once. The eyes remained open.

They sat silently on the porch for a time. Then Darryl told Walt to get a shovel and dig a hole where he wanted it. Walt started back from the barn but halted a moment at the sight of his father staring dumbly at Henry's body. He had been crying after his father shot the dog, but the tears had been replaced by a queer, sad lucidity. He saw his mother and father and the long tunnel of years stretched before him. He saw the trap of circumstance and emotion, the moil of egocentric energy looking backward and forward, regret and anticipation, that none avoid.

He remembered a word his grandfather, according to Letty, had repeated often as he grew near to dying. The world was somehow "irredeemable" the old preacher had said.

A little later Darryl and Walt found Letty cowering in the woodshed with her hands over her ears to keep out the sound of the shooting.

The Seeker, the Snake
and the Baba

As a snake perceived in the twilight may prove to be a rope (merely
a harmless rope, yet it was taken for a snake and inspired fear),
even so the world, which inspires fear and desire, may be caused
to vanish.

Hindu Proverb

The heat stunned him. In the square outside Puri Station
beggars, brandishing their stumps, swarmed like maggots. A
pyre smouldered by the river as kites swung expectantly on the
thermals. Bearded mystics, caked in blood and ashes, skewered
with nails, staggered in ecstasy. By the taxi stand, a slender
youth, naked, his eyes hooded, teased a pair of snakes with a
bulbous flute. Malory shuddered. After an hour's drive, the
cabman announced, "The ashram of Sri Govinda Baba. Very
famous place. Many Americans are coming." "I am English,"
said Malory. "Also many English," said the cabman. "See,
master, the river is almost dry here. The birds drop out of the

trees. The Baba is expecting you?" "I think not."

•

During the day the cobras slept . . .

•

It was not his fault; the woman had put a spell on him with her love. Women. Jody, Ursula, Andrea. Though he perceived that they were all aspects of one woman: his mistresses, his muses, his graces, his fates, his victims. Of the three, Ursula was the key. Jody was the practical one. Independent. She wanted no ties. When she became pregnant, she moved in with him so that he could support her confinement. Then she fled. Andrea was Dutch and placid; he married her. It was Ursula, the middle one, who caused the trouble. She had an abortion; the baby was sacrificed so as not to chain him down. He didn't exactly tell her to do it. He disappeared (with Andrea) when she went to the clinic so that he would not be there to influence her at the last. Then she seemed to think she had a hold on him, as though their love had a name now she had christened it with blood. He had a friend relay the news that he would be married. It had to be quick; Andrea was pregnant by this time. The night before the wedding he went to Ursula. Her eyes accused him, but her voice was soft and resigned. She said, "It's not me I pity. It's you. You have to live with her." And she wept tears like petals on their pillow when they made love. (No fear this time. Her wise doctor said, "A healthy young woman like you ought to be on the pill.") The tuft of hair between her legs had not grown back since the operation, it all happened so fast. After the wedding she went away though he had wanted her to stay near him. She went away not to be free as Jody had done but to give him a chance to make a marriage. She knew he would never settle down as long as she was around. She had her nose straightened and murdered love with work and light diversion. But something remained amiss; the doctor diagnosed a malignancy and operated. He telephoned when he heard. "My

72

seed is bad." "Nonsense," she said. "I've lost my hair." "If it doesn't work, how long?" he asked. "Two years," she said. "You can have a lot of fun in two years," he said. Her friends had wept when she told them. "That's just Kenneth Malory," she said, "inept and cruel." She loved him still.

•

During the day the cobras slept in the river-bank gardens of the ashram where the gravel was cool and moist. At night they came into the houses to hunt for mice.

•

It was not his fault; his father had made him in his image. The two of them. For there was a sister, and with her he sometimes thought he could truly love. ("You had better go, Malory," said Ursula's stepfather. "Her mother is frail and I'm not up to the journey myself. Besides, the telegram is meant for you. It's addressed to us, but it's meant for you. I'll pay, of course. We should like her buried here.") She had been engaged four times and each time had broken it off just before the wedding. She was a small, pretty woman who worked in a travel agency. (Practice in evasion and flight, he thought.) She was open and kind, but when a man pushed her too far she would tighten up and hurl him back. He said, "We are the same, you and I. We cannot commit ourselves to love." This once she defied him. "Not true, Kenny. We are not the same. I can love, believe me I can love, but I will never let a man rule me. You are like Daddy, you prove yourself by getting babies." Ursula had said, "You don't know what you want. But I think you are afraid of hurting women. It's the guilt that drives you on." (Too true, he thought. The guilt for Ursula's baby made him marry poor Andrea. Though Andrea was an afterthought, a mistake. He had intended to stop with Ursula.) Jody had called him a misogynist. "Maybe you're gay underneath," she said. "I think you hate us, try to drive us down into the earth, the blood and the pain. It's the sadism of childbirth that excites you." It was not his fault; his father was

73

a drunk and a wife-beater who lived mostly away from home. He had been home the day Malory's mother was sent to the hospital with a 'female complaint.' The old man refused to sign the papers for an operation. He refused on the grounds that it would make him less of a man in bed with her. So she died. ("KENNETH, COME QUICKLY," said the telegram like a revelation.)

•

He was not sure there was a snake in the hut. Other nights he had heard rustling in the kra logs and bamboo of the walls. He held his terror, fluttering like a moth against his ribs, his teeth chattering a travesty of castanets. The night sucked up his breath.

•

"They came by bus from Kabul after the rains," said the German woman who had looked after Ursula. "She was already sick." At first, Malory had been angry. He had sent the German woman away and ordered the taxi to Puri to fetch fresh food and a doctor. By the time the doctor arrived, he had managed to clean the worst of the filth from the hut and air the blankets Ursula was using. She was emaciated, her hair hung in rat-tails, she could not close her lips over her teeth, she was incontinent. He found needle tracks on her arms and legs, erupted, almost gangrenous, like snake bites. The doctor, who spoke little English, pointed to the punctures and shrugged his shoulders. "Kaput," he said. "Poison." When he washed her, Malory had to steel himself to touch the strange waxy skin and bend the flaccid joints. He did not understand how a white woman could be allowed to languish in such misery. The ashram disgusted him: the rag-tag huts where the European disciples lived, the crowds of followers milling at the gate, the white-clad attendants with their buttery cheeks, the stench, the heat. He couldn't even find water clean enough to rinse the fouled bed-clothes, but had to buy a kettle and firewood for boiling. Once, briefly, while he was moistening her lips with a rag, her eyes opened and she saw him. Her look was cold; it seemed to pierce him with the iciness of remorse. As he dried her belly he touched her sex experimentally. "The doctor scraped me out like a cream carton," she had said. "No more baby panics for me." In the evening, the German woman returned. "I lied," she said. "There was no other, no man. She . . . she took care of me." "You were lovers," he said. "No. No. You misunderstand. I am a sinful person." She showed him the marks on her arms. "Ursula helped me to stop." "But she took drugs as well," he said. "Yes, after. We went to Afghanistan for the drugs. When the Russians invaded we came south. When she took the drugs she would sigh and whisper, 'Shiva, Lord of Sleep.' We came here to find peace."

•

On the cot in the night he sweated with fever. He had forgotten to mix purification tablets in his drinking water. He was afraid to leave the cot to go to the humid ditch which served as a latrine for the foreigners' compound. The pain of cramps, dehydration and his enforced stillness had driven him nearly delirious. He imaged the black swaying body, the spectacle patterns on its hood peering at him, just there beyond his feet. The void enclosed him at the point of contact. He was enveloped in an emptiness that moved like the body of a snake.

•

The ashram was made dangerous by the proximity of migrating elephant herds. For Malory it was a nightmare of heat, death pyres and bearded ascetics drinking their own urine by the gates. He watched Ursula, her face made beautiful by suffering, and told himself that character is fate, that every human being is treacherous to another, that men only dream of union. "She is happy," said the German woman. "Memory was such a torture to her." She did not die; she merely continued. He rose late each day because it disgusted him to go to the ditch which served as a toilet when the Indians were there. Most of the foreigners arrived after mid-morning, unless they were ill, and squatted at decent intervals staring tactfully ahead. After visiting

75

the ditch he would wash carefully, despite the trouble of preparing the water, before attending to Ursula. Twice a day in the morning and the afternoon the Baba would appear at the gates of the ashram with his closest disciples. The pilgrims, who at times mustered in the thousands, would rush to the spot in an uproar of devotion. Around the gate was a low hill which served as an amphitheatre. The crowds would settle on the incline and the Baba would begin to meditate. No one had ever heard him speak to the pilgrims, though sometimes he searched among them with eyes that were at once alarmingly direct and peacefully muddy. Here and there he would transfix a visitor with his stare. This happened to Malory, the second day, as he stood upon the hill near the back of the multitude. The Baba's gaze, placid yet peremptory, even insolent, chilled him and filled him with anger. It seemed to him that the holy man was contemptible in his detachment, that he fed on the suffering endured in his name, that all India was suffering to earn his redemption. After the observances, the crowd had dispersed in search of food. This was a constant preoccupation since, with native impracticality, the ashram had been built miles from any town. There were no stores, no sewage facilities, and, except for the river in which the bodies of men and animals mixed indiscriminately, only a few wells for water. There were several carts at the gate which sold Indian food, but the foreigners generally did not trust the sanitation. They traded and hoarded amongst themselves in an atmosphere of despair and suspicion. In the evening, returning to the hut with some cans of American soup, Malory had found Eva murmuring to herself at the foot of Ursula's cot, the air heavy with the smell of burning joss. "You must be mad to be taken in by this fraud," he said. "He is a saint," she said. "He can foretell the future." "She wanted to live her life in a dream," he said, looking down at the dying woman. "She wanted you to come," said Eva, "to rescue her from this. She never accepted separation. But she understood that one must relinquish to truly love." "Ursula was a masochist," said Malory. "A woman's masochism comes from her maternal instinct," said Eva. "It is not a perversion. A mother suffers, gives, feeds . . . ."

76

•

After a few days at the ashram, no one was completely well. Women missed their periods; men shook with fever. Malory watched the Indians burning their dead on pyres by the river with bodies and logs piled neatly in alternating layers. When the ashes were cool, the remains were pushed over the bank. There were always more dead. Sometimes it seemed as though there were more bodies than living people so that he assumed the corpses were brought from far away for cremation at the holy place. Everywhere there was a stench of human excrement, saffron, burning bodies, ghee butter used in sacrifice and un-washed humanity. In the afternoons after meditation the Baba performed the ceremony of the holy ashes. He would walk to the edge of the crowd and, twirling his hand in the air above his head, would materialize a pinkish fine-grained ash, almost like smoke as it fell from his palm. The devout held up their arms to receive the holy gift. It was said to cure illness if eaten or pro-cure great spiritual benefit if retained in a charm pouch around the neck. The Baba's inner circle was in the business of selling the ashes to the pilgrims in tiny folded envelopes. The holy one could change the weather, bring rain, Malory was told. One day he had walked in the sea and a necklace of precious stones had miraculously appeared about his ankle, the waves' offering to God incarnate. The previous year he had levitated at the prime minister's swearing-in. Evenings he could sometimes be seen driving golf balls toward the river from the temple roof, his whispy beard floating about his cheeks, his white robes hiked up on his shoulders. Malory found many men willing to help him achieve an audience with Sri Govinda Baba. They took his money, as alms, and like attorneys proceeded to put the machinery in motion. In Malory's case, the machinery appeared to be perpetual and circular for the Baba would not see him.

•

It was worse when he could detect no sound at all. It meant that the snake was coiled quite near, waiting. If he but swung his hand out to

77

*touch the table by the bed, it would strike. A dart of fangs in the night.
He dared not put his foot to the floor lest the snake be there.*

•

In a dream the Baba appeared to him. "What is it you seek?"
the holy man asked. "Release, master." "You know the
Bhuvaneshvara?" asked Baba. "It is not far from here." "I have
seen it on the map," Malory replied. "There is a temple called
the Rajrani built in ancient times by a wealthy courtesan for her
king. If you go, Englishman, into the lightless holy of holies in
the Rajrani you will find no image or symbol whatsoever. The
people say that when the king entered the sanctuary the
presence there found was the courtesan herself." Baba began
to giggle at the conclusion of his tale. "I don't understand," said
Malory. At this the saint began to laugh heartily.

•

The next day, leaving Eva to watch over Ursula, Malory hiked
to the Rajrani of Bhuvaneshvara to see the whore's temple. A
crowd had gathered at the entrance to the sanctuary where a
group of ascetics and fakirs were performing. There was a man
with a basket of cobras. He had laid the snakes out on a hemp
mat and was serenading them with a flute. Some of the snakes
had coiled and spread their hoods and were swaying back and
forth in time to the music. Others lay in the sunlight, blinking
and flicking their tongues, oozing off the mat in sluggish attempts
at escape. Without halting his playing, the fakir would reach down
with one hand and return the snake to his mat. From time to
time one of the coiled cobras would dart its head forward in
a strike, but the blow was awkward and easily avoided by the
man with the flute. "You are fascinated by the snakes?" asked
a man in a white dhoti among the spectators. "It is like bull-
fighting really." The speaker was not one of the ascetics. He
had an accent that was very correct, very English. "The cobra
is rather slow and dull-witted and cannot hear at all. The music
is for our benefit not the snake's. He only watches the motion

78

of the flute. That is what he strikes at. And of course he is not a quick snake like the viper." "But surely their fangs are pulled," said Malory. "No. No. It is quite real. I dare say he has been bitten. One develops an immunity, I'm told. But there are so many snakes and they come into the houses. Many people die each year. It's horrible, they say, pain, numbness, loss of co-ordination, incontinence, convulsions." "They aren't exterminated?" Malory interrupted. "Heavens, no! Life is sacred to us. Also the snakes help keep down pests. Why look so disgusted? I am told that Americans have ophitic cults where the devout handle rattlesnakes. The snake is a very old, very revered symbol in all cultures." Haunted by the image of the black wriggling bodies on the hemp mat, Malory entered the sanctuary. Inside, the temple was dark. He could not see to place his feet. The feeling of apprehension grew as he shuffled down a row of bare stone steps. Something rustled beneath him. Perhaps he had dislodged a pebble. He could see nothing. His heart raced. He found that he could not move his feet forward. Abruptly, he turned and fled, rushing up the steps to the delight of the man in the dhoti who had waited by the entrance. "What are you afraid of?" he shouted. "The dark! The king's whore! You see it is not walls that hinder us. It is the power of our own thoughts. These spikes," he said, indicating a holy man covered in ashes and blood, steel spikes driven through his thighs, "these spikes are no bother when one knows the power of the human soul. Neuroses, all those so-called psychological illnesses of the West, however sad they may seem, are but acts of belief."

•

What sound did the snake make dragging its heaviness across the sand? What sound did Death make? What sound the Holy Ghost? He was certain of a presence that was not a presence so much as a void, an emptiness, just beyond his ability to sense in the darkness. He imagined again the black weaving body, the eyes of its hood staring. I have a visitor, he thought, covering his face. He cried out. And the void sucked up his cries.

•

For a week Ursula declined, yet lingered, muffled in coma. Malory discovered his clothing infested with body lice. One day he neglected to mix purification tablets with the water he drank. "You were delirious last night," said the German woman. "I dreamed about the snakes," he said. She nodded. "I also when I close my eyes. Once I desired nothing more than to live the life she led. Now Shiva has come to me in my sleep." It was on his return from the Rajrani that he had discovered the first penitents before the hut, the first saucers of burning ghee set near the door. Now there were fifty or more every day, beggars, invalids, the self-tortured. They had festooned the lintel with garlands of flowers. They had brought food which he would not eat. While they demanded nothing, they persisted, quietly, amid the flies and dust. Their presence was a mystery only Eva dared to interpret. "They worship her," she said. "She was the innocent who was always suffering." To Malory, they seemed only to be waiting. Shuddering inwardly, he told himself he was disgusted and no longer cared. It seemed to him that India was wearing away his civilizing resolve. He felt himself slipping into a form of madness that was simultaneously frightening and seductive. His anger and discomfort had become his justification.

•

The Baba woke him coming to speak with Ursula. "She will die before morning," he said. At first Malory could not understand. The hut was full of retainers wearing bells and chanting mantras. They bore oil lamps, held high, and peeked fearfully into corners as though looking for ghosts. Sri Govinda Baba walked directly to Ursula's cot, knelt and began an ecstatic prayer. A young man followed, carrying a framed painting of the holy man's annunciation: the boy, Govinda, asleep on his bed with a large cobra watching over him, just as his mother had found them that holy morning. Now past sixty, the Baba looked fat and healthy. His cunning eyes devoured the sleeping Ursula. He snapped his fingers. A bowl was provided. And he dabbed her face with a paste of ashes and butter. Malory tried to protest. "She had pain here," said the Baba, pointing to her heart. "Now it has vanished. Her illness was but a candle in the sun of Shiva." To Malory, the Indian seemed to embody the split nature of the androgyne, male and female, father and mother. "She is the goddess of all things which the vigour of living destroys. She is Shakti." Malory wanted to reply but the old man imposed respect. He continued, pointing to the open door where the worshippers had gathered in silence. "They understand. It is the bhairava, the terror, the cult name of Shiva." He fingered the infected wounds on her arms. He gazed at Malory. "She came to find peace and discovered the power of Shiva. She gave herself to him, Shakti the divine, the fecundating force. She gave herself." "She took drugs," said Malory bitterly. "She let the cobra strike her," said the Baba. Malory felt the hair on the back of his neck rise. His throat spasmed, making a dry clicking sound like a rattle. "It came in the night. There! There!" cried the Baba, gesturing at the walls. "Mahadeva of the thousand names, Shiva, the void, the eternal corpse, the terrible destroyer; Shiva, Lord of Sleep."

•

It was not his fault. Nothing had ever been his fault. Driven from the hut by the press of believers, the drone of prayers, and the sickening sweetness of the joss, he had spent the night on his feet in the open. Before sunrise he found a man with a car who could drive him to Puri. The doctor who had treated Ursula at the beginning was a Moslem. He was up early, performing his ritual ablutions, when Malory knocked on his door. "She lives?" he asked, with disbelief. Malory shook the doctor by the shoulders. "Poison! You said poison! My God, it was the drugs, the needles. Another boy died while I was there. Hepatitis. He had hepatitis from the needles." The doctor backed away, brushing down his sleeves. "No, poison," he said. His hand darted, the first and second fingers extended like fangs. "Ssst! Ssst! Naja . . . cobra." "What about her cancer?" cried Malory in desperation. The doctor shrugged. Malory slumped in a chair. "I want to move the body," he said. "I must return it to England."

81

"A month," said the doctor. "Papers, police, the government."
He shrugged once more. Returning to the ashram, Malory found
the area around the hut deserted. Eva met him at the door, weeping. The odour of death and putrefaction was heavy in the air.
Inside, the hut was empty. "Was it true?" he asked, his voice
taut with horror. "Did she do what he said?" Eva nodded. "Where
have they taken her?" The German woman extended her hand
towards the river. A pyre was being erected. The bank was teem-
ing with Indians looking like brown insects in the harsh sunlight.
A little to one side, surrounded by his retinue, Sri Govinda Baba
sat erect in a jeep, painted pink and covered in flowers. "You
can't," shouted Malory when he reached the jeep. "She must
go back to England with me." The Baba, his eyes closed in
meditation, took no notice. But a middle-aged man touched
Malory gently on the arm and said, "It is better this way, master.
She had begun to decay even before she ceased to breathe."
He pointed toward the sun. "It is hot. A policeman has ordered
the cremation as a sanitary measure." The man's voice was soft
and reassuring. What he said seemed reasonable, especially
when he mentioned the policeman, although Malory had not
seen a policeman since his arrival at the ashram. Yet he wanted
to protest. Something needed to be said. He shook off the
speaker's hand angrily. The man stepped back. "Men die
because they cannot join the beginning and the end," he said.
Immediately a second voice behind Malory repeated the words.
"Men die because they cannot join the beginning and the end."
A mournful sigh, the totality of a thousand exhalations, emanated
from the river bank. As Malory turned, the flames roared upward.
The Baba's jeep coughed into life and turned toward the ashram
gate where the line of food carts stood waiting. Even at a distance
Malory could feel the heat of the pyre. He felt its radiance on
his chest and his forehead. The flames danced in his eyes. He
held up his hands, feeling the warmth on his palms stretched
toward the flames, and in the pit of his belly he felt a knot. His
mouth opened as if to vomit, and all the breath that was in him
seemed to rush out in one mad cry.

•

During the day the cobras slept in the river-bank gardens of the ashram where the gravel was cool and moist. At night they came into the houses to hunt for mice.

He was not sure there was a snake in the hut. Other nights he had heard rustling in the kra logs and bamboo of the walls. He held his terror, fluttering against his ribs, his teeth chattering a travesty of castanets. The night sucked up his breath.

He thought it must be the fever that made him so sensitive to the presence and the sound that was almost a negative as though it sucked up and annihilated every other sound. He lay awake, absorbed in listening for the undulating black body dragging itself across the sandy floor. He should not have forgotten the purification tablets. He had to go to the ditch. What sound did the snake make oozing across the sand? What sound did Death make? What sound the Holy Ghost? He imagined the snake emerging downward from the wattles of the roof, lengthening in the emptiness of night, then sagging with the weight of its body and drop-ping with a lush heaviness to his bed.

Something touches his foot.
Malory screams.
The snake sucks up his screams.

83

Heartsick

"My eighth husband, Putzi, hated . . . ."

Constanza Heboyan, millionairess and one-time owner of the Ever-Ready, a brothel in Tonopah, Nevada, tried to remember what Putzi had hated. Nothing came to mind. Now that she thought of it, she wasn't even sure she had married Putzi.

Constanza was sitting alone on a stone bench at the foot of the garden where the River Ulm cut the property of the Karl-Gustav Institute for the Elderly Insane into two pieces. Beyond the river was a park (there was a stone footbridge), but no one ever went there. No one Constanza knew could walk that far. Past the institute wall there rose a large tree-covered hill which the Germans called Kaiserstuhl. Constanza rendered this loosely as "King Shit" but no one else got the joke because no one else spoke English. And she knew they weren't German; they were really Austrian.

She remembered now that she hadn't married Putzi. If she had, her name would have been Respighi instead of Heboyan. Heboyan was the nice Armenian ship owner who used to pout when she refused to get out of bed to look at his little boats. The money was Heboyan's. Putzi came later, when she had to pay to get laid.

She sighed and clutched the pit of her belly (rubbing dry sticks to make a fire) and imagined riding around the room on Putzi's cock. Biting his cheeks till the blood came. His prosthetic boot coming CLOMP-clomp in unison with his hard-on. She shouting: *Ho Hephaestos! Ha Vulcan, my crippled god! Fuck me, you ninny!*

(He had lost a foot in the war; Hephaestos—because he was poet laureate of the Communist Metal Workers League in Perugia. There are reasons for everything.)

CLOMP-clomp. CLOMP-clomp.

That Putzi!

●

In the papers that morning she had read of a girl made pregnant in a terrible rape. The girl had taken a knife and stabbed herself through the stomach to kill the baby in her womb.

Sometimes strong measures are necessary . . . .

I knew you would understand, Putzi.

She had confronted Gar Osten as he returned from his daily constitutional (from the institute door to the edge of the patio and back, supporting himself on a four-footed walker).

"It is generally recognized," she said, "that orgasm probably doesn't increase the heart rate more than climbing two flights of stairs."

He gazed at her uncomprehendingly (all brawn and no brain . . . a real mensch), a string of drool running from his chin to his collar. (Got to make him while he's still alive. Fucking dead men doesn't count.)

"You see, darling, you have nothing to fear. It's perfectly safe."

He cocked his head like a dog in an effort to understand.

"Are you deaf?"

Gar Osten grinned enthusiastically and began to manoeuvre his walker between Constanza and the door-jamb. At the same moment she let go one of her canes and made a grab for his trouser front (piss-stained, prostate the size of a baseball).

86

"I hope you don't think I'm one of those aggressive women . . ."

Gar Osten twisted frantically in his walker, his eyes rolling with fear. (Did you see his hips move? she thought. The man is still capable!) She missed his crotch and went crashing to the flagstones with a concussion that knocked her false teeth out of her mouth.

". . . but I feel we have so little time."

She raised her head and straightened her glasses in time to see all six legs of him scuttling crab-like towards the married patients' wing, his breath coming in grunts (HUNH-hunh, HUNH-hunh), his tall thin (that's not skin; God spray-painted his bones) body bent like a bow over the walker as he fled. (So distinguished, she thought. So Nordic. Even if he is incontinent.) At the far door, Berte, his wife, waiting to meet him, looking anxiously over his shoulder at . . . .

•

Connie, what are you in here for?

Oh, Putzi, I'm ashamed. I exposed myself in front of a bus-load of tourists bound for the Salzburger Festival. I am told I ruined their holiday.

And the doctors? What do they call it?

Exhibitionism, nymphomania, senile dementia, despair. "The appetitive component of the patient's eroto-genital function shows marked development for a woman of eighty-three." Don't look at me, Putzi. My cunt's in good nick, but my implants have slipped.

Like grapes that wither for want of pressing.

Caro mio, you were a bad poet. I suffer from old loves.

•

Constanza had intercepted the couple following their 11 a.m. consultation with Dr. Goedelfinger.

"My dear Gar Osten," she began. "I understand that, despite the recent revolution in sexual mores, some men remain fastidious in matters relating to conjugation. I perceive that the unfortunate incident this morning has given you an incorrect impression . . . ."

His head tossing, eyes sliding wildly from side to side, nostrils

87

flaring steed-like, Berte tugging at his elbow, Gar Osten jerked and rolled his walker past Constanza and down the corridor.

"Madame!" she shouted. (She had always been able to attract attention to herself when it was necessary.) "Release that man at once. Don't you think he's a trifle old for sporting events?"

The Ostens stopped and blinked at Constanza over their shoulders.

"Thank you. As I was saying, I am in perfect concord with the Pope on the doctrine of the spiritual regeneration of the hymen. (When she was younger, every time was the first time.) You see before you a chaste widow (technically true, she thought, since all her husbands were dead; divorce no longer binds us after we pass the gate), seeking fraternal association with . . ."

"Was? Was? What is she saying?" asked Berte in German.

". . . with a mature . . . ."

Constanza faltered. (What the fuck!) Abruptly, she turned and hobbled to the patio to smell the chrysanthemums. All the flowers were suspended in haloes of light (cataracts, she decided) and reminded her of Berte Osten's moist bespectacled eyes.

●

Putzi, why do you seem so wistful?

I am dead.

What an absurd man! Everything on the grand scale! When you took a crap, you acted as though you'd created the world; when you had a cold, it was lung cancer; when you wrote a poem, you were Homer for a day; and when we made love, you acted as though you'd had a religious experience. Now you tell me you're dead.

Nevertheless, it's true.

Perhaps you're right. I may have forgotten. Since I underwent electro-shock therapy, my memory has been somewhat selective.

We are all yesterdays who haunt each other's lives like ghosts.

The doctors stopped when they found I attained sexual arousal during the treatment.

●

The River Ulm pulsed hypnotically a few feet from where Constanza sat. It was evening. She imagined trout hiding in hollows, waiting for the stars to come out.

"My eighth husband, Putzi, hated . . . ."

It was on the tip of her tongue. It frustrated her that she could not remember. Her spirit (or was it her heart?) fluttered vainly against the bars of her (rib) cage, and it seemed to Constanza that remembering was somehow the key to . . . .

Putzi, what was it you hated so much?

You already know.

(Which, of course, wasn't an answer, she thought.)

She did recall meeting Putzi in the *rioni*, in a political bar below street level in the Via delle Volte della Pace by the Etruscan wall. The car had thrown a rod on the highway to Rimini; her chauffeur was assisting a local mechanic. She had wandered into the Galleria Nazionale, admired Perugino's Dead Christ, His livid flesh against a black background, and rushed out (as usual) needing a man.

He stood on a table, smoking a Russian cigarette, sipping claret, declaiming his municipal epic *Maleteste Baglione* to a crowd of comrades hiding out from their wives. And she quietly stunned them all, dealing ten $100 bills at his feet like Tarot cards and looking deep into his eyes while he spoke.

Putzi stared at the money, then at Constanza (her intensity, her strange once-beauty, is still prophetic), then at the money, then at . . . (a tremor palpitates her breast; is it of desire, of fear?).

It was like peering into a whirlpool. I had to jump.

I took out my teeth and blew you behind a wine cask.

And when we returned, the workers cheered you like Gramsci, like Garibaldi!

After you were dead, Putzi, I loved you.

•

She had waited until Berte left him to visit the W.C. (in such wise doth matter ever betray the spirit, she thought) then approached Gar Osten in a mood of philosophical detachment.

"How sick I am of civilized relationships," she said with a sigh.

He was seated beside a window, his walker out of reach. He could not rise. He was looking at a dead bird on the lawn.

"I *long* for passion, for love with a little blood in it!"

Gar Osten yawned nervously, a spike of drool launched itself from his lower lip.

"Oh darling, wives are such vestigial affairs," she went on. "Each day is a carbon copy of the last; a marriage gets fainter and fainter . . . ."

"Roor!" said Gar Osten, hoarsely. He pointed one feeble skeletal finger.

"It's a dead bird," Constanza observed dryly.

His breath bellowed in stertorous drafts. HUNH-hunh. HUNH-hunh. (And she thought, What a great heart! The more soul, the more suffering. If only he weren't so . . . so . . . oblivious.)

She tried once more: "Please, Gar, listen to me. If we are not to enslave others with our love, there must be a limit to the claims of attachment." She took his chin in her hand and turned it so that she could peer into his face. (He looked better when she held his mouth closed.) "In this world, *Liebling*, we must commit love like a crime as a litmus of its truth."

Gar Osten caught sight of Berte marching towards them, her fists pumping like pistons in an attempt to increase her pace. His eyes began to oscillate from woman to woman. His body shook in spasms.

"What do you want? What do you do with my husband?" demanded the wife in breathless German.

"Only a little love, darling. A little love, or any reasonable fac-simile." (English)

"What does she say? What does she say?" (German)

HUNH-hunh. HUNH-hunh. (?)

"It's a dead bird," said Constanza, wearily, and she moved slowly away, nodding like an ibis feeding in shallow water.

•

She sighed. Her heart tugged. Memory tapped an old vein. She recalled a moment when the shadow touched him so. In the ogive, framed, back-lit by a harsh Mediterranean sun, Putzi hovered uncertainly, still and separate, caught in the tension and sadness of incomplete gesture. *My eighth husband* . . . (like a dancer in a photograph) *hated* . . . . And the scene had stamped itself on the stubborn fabric of her consciousness, beautiful and enigmatic, like some flower whose name she had forgotten.

●

Restless, at lunch she had ignored the clear soup and paté to deliver a lecture (for staff and ambulatory patients) on the proper maintenance of interment facilities for the beloved departed. At her 1 p.m. consultation she informed Dr. Goedelfinger that in English a *pen is a penis*. She told him a joke about a reincarnated psychologist who sang, as his soul drifted back to earth: "I'm glad I'm not Jung anymore." And then she tried to explain for him the significance of Maleteste (Bad Balls, she had translated; Putzi nearly splitting his forehead on a tabletop, laughing) Baglione, the warrior who handled his cannon ineptly and sounded the retreat on the point of victory.

Old Maleteste (she must have said), old Bad Balls, old scamp, old scalliwag, scapegrace, turncoat, rake-hell, old *ame-de-boue*, old *passe-partout*, old rip, old fallen angel. Old white-livered poltroon. Old pessimist. Old shadow-shuffler. Old passion pit, old lust pot, old leader of men and molester of young horses. A man, in short, of incalculable zeal and confused purposes. A man, in short . . . .

(Constanza was aware that Dr. Goedelfinger had fallen asleep thus rendering himself, if possible, less pervious than usual to her tangential soliloquies.)

And Putzi's strange ironic poem about the betrayal of the Florentines. When Maleteste brought unreasonable demands to cloak his treachery, and the men of Florence gave in, even sending a messenger to confirm the bargain while Bad Balls did bumplay with a Siennese *castrato*. The old sinner slew the herald himself with Toledo steel and turned his guns on his allies' city. Writing new chapters of infamy.

Yet, on the day of his triumph, when he measured the streets of Perugia leading twin lion cubs, a Pope's reward for his connivance, Maleteste's people cheered and wept. And, for the five nights preceding his death by syphilis a year later, a meteor blazed over Monte Malbe, and the long last day he spoke in prophecies.

●

*Oh, Putzi, I've got the panics. I can't fuck, I can't sleep, I can't eat. I cannot
even lie down in the dark without thinking of it. (What?) They give me pills
for my heart, pills for my liver, pills to breathe and pills to piss. I haven't had
a decent crap in three weeks. I sweat like a pig in my sheets as soon as the
lights go out. I need a pill to make me young again and all they give me are
anti-depressants. If I can't feel anything, I might as well be dead. Once I was
beautiful; now I am . . . .*

Like a rose crushed too often in the book of life.

*Exactly. But you always knew me best. Why did you go out that day (in
the archway, framed)? Why did you leave me? I could have saved you even
then. But no, you had to act like you were in some damned opera. Oh, Putzi,
I am unwell. I feel all inside-out and empty.*

●

What a past, she thought. I have survived. And furthermore
I am horny and vindictive. Does the fire never die?

She had stolen old Kuiper's wheelchair while he lay helpless
in four inches of lukewarm bathwater and locked herself in the
service elevator with a half-dozen hampers of soiled linen and
a carton of Picayunes shipped specially from New Orleans by
a zealous beneficiary. (She made water on the seat without noticing, her spindly shanks propped on Kuiper's footrests.) For an
hour she meditated, flicking her butts into the laundry with cynical
precision.

The Sybil of Cumae in her Grotto.

Putzi, you're just like all the rest of the men I screwed.

How's that?

You're dead and not a damn bit of use!

Smashing an alarm box with her cane, she had sent the
smouldering car to the basement and made her way through the
ensuing evacuation to the married patients' wing, rolling the
wheelchair before her like a barrow. (This is too much, she
thought. Someone must put a stop to it.)

She whistled nervously (*Fidelio*); her chest pounded (we always
run faster when we have lost our way). She found the Ostens'

door ajar, but the old couple had made no attempt to escape. Berte was seated. Gar had fallen to his knees with his face pressed between her slack breasts like a frightened boy (pathetic couple).

"Run for your life," cried Constanza. "I'll save old spaghetti legs."

"Was?" whispered Berte, her wide eyes like blossoms, her arms twined round her husband's head.

"Run!" cried Constanza. (What a girl has to go through to get fucked, she thought.)

A tear fell from Berte's nose as she slowly shook her head from side to side (like a turtle). And her fat white hand reached to caress Gar's hair (his scalp crimson and flaky as a knuckle) and press him closer to her heart.

Constanza hesitated. "Why don't you run away?" she asked. She watched the pale squat fingers combing the old unwise hair of the man and felt a sly nothingness plucking at her elbow.

What do you suppose it was? she asked.

The foetus of doubt.

(*Love, love, she thought.*)

It seemed to Constanza that she saw Berte for the first time. Those tender eyes did not reproach her. Those arms did not exclude her. What she saw revealed in the charm and beauty of gesture was a world of love, pity, forgiveness and charity. ("This is too much," her voices said.)

Sadly, she turned and left the room. The smoke was already beginning to clear. Forgetting her infirmity, she walked all the way to the patio before collapsing in a heap on the flagstones.

•

The first stars appeared in Ursus and Orion. From time to time, Constanza caught sight of Dr. Goedelfinger's anxious face like a pale blue balloon in the garden window. He was watching (for all he knew the Heboyan endowment hung in the balance), just as the trout were watching from the water, just as Putzi was watching, just as Connie was watching herself.

"My eighth husband, Putzi, hated . . . dying."

And she remembered him now: one of those gentle mystic

93

Umbrian souls with a cock like a Clydesdale and a price on his head. That night she had taken a room in the Albergo Deneau off the Corso Vanucci. She had promised to publish his poems in deluxe editions. And for a week she kept him there, feasting on his Italian sausage.

Outside, he had told her, they waited for him, hooded and armed. They were angry, he said. "Art opposes systems," he said. "Irony deforms ideology." She begged him to let her help. (The chauffeur waited in the alley with the engine running.) On the last day, Connie knew. It was in the air, and in his eyes, a sad heaviness there, a wistfulness. He had performed (as usual) like a stallion, had made her come over and over, until she lay dazed and trembling, boneless and lazy. Then, dressing, he had gone out (in an archway, framed).

●

There was a bomb in your moped.

It took my best parts.

At first I thought, "This can't be real. It's just another prank. All that blood. No one has that much blood." You didn't really think they'd do it, did you?

I admit I misjudged them.

And it wasn't the Red Brigades or the CIA. It was a man you owed money to.

I never said I was perfect.

I was prevented from attending your funeral because it turned out you had a wife and nine children, all of whom I have supported from that moment to this. They curse Heboyan. Though perhaps it was natural not to understand what was between us. Putzi, you were the best, even if I had to pay.

In life we always lose more than we plunder. And, as the French say, even a beautiful woman cannot give more than she has.

That's enough darling. Don't try my patience.

I am waiting, Connie. I am waiting.

●

She trailed her fingers lightly across the tips of her breasts, saw the stars, the trout and the Kaiserstuhl, smelled the flowers in the garden behind her, remembered husbands and lovers long gone, and sighed a little in a way that was neither happy nor unhappy. Putzi was right, she knew. It was time to say that was that, to make distinctions, to put a nail in the lid of the coffin of her past, into which she was falling continually from the present. But nothing seemed urgent any more. Briefly, she had a vision. Old Kuiper lying naked in his bath. A troop of angels landing in a field like butterflies. And Berte Osten's eyes.

Tomorrow, or the next day, Constanza thought, she would walk over the stone bridge and see what lay hidden amongst the trees beyond the river.

Dog Attempts to Drown Man in Saskatoon

My wife and I decide to separate, and then suddenly we are almost happy together. The pathos of our situation, our private and unique tragedy, lends romance to each small act. We see everything in the round, the facets as opposed to the flat banality that was wedging us apart. When she asks me to go to the Mendel Art Gallery Sunday afternoon, I do not say no with the usual mounting irritation that drives me into myself. I say yes and some hardness within me seems to melt into a pleasant sadness. We look into each other's eyes and realize with a start that we are looking for the first time because it is the last. We are both thinking, "Who is this person to whom I have been married? What has been the meaning of our relationship?" These are questions we have never asked ourselves; we have been a blind couple groping with each other in the dark. Instead of saying to myself, "Not the art gallery again! What does she care about art? She has no education. She's merely bored and on Sunday afternoon in Saskatoon the only place you can go is the old sausage-maker's mausoleum of art!" instead of putting up arguments, I think, "Poor Lucy,

97

pursued by the assassins of her past, unable to be still. Perhaps if I had her memories I also would be unable to stay in on a Sunday afternoon." Somewhere that cretin Pascal says that all our problems stem from not being able to sit quietly in a room alone. If Pascal had had Lucy's mother, he would never have written anything so foolish. Also, at the age of nine, she saw her younger brother run over and killed by a highway roller. Faced with that, would Pascal have written anything? (Now I am defending my wife against Pascal! A month ago I would have used the same passage to bludgeon her.)

•

Note. Already this is not the story I wanted to tell. That is buried, gone, lost—its action fragmented and distorted by inexact recollection. Directly it was completed, it had disappeared, gone with the past into that strange realm of suspended animation, that coatrack of despair, wherein all our completed acts await, gathering dust, until we come for them again. I am trying to give you the truth, though I could try harder, and only refrain because I know that that way leads to madness. So I offer an approximation, a shadow play, such as would excite children, full of blind spots and irrelevant adumbrations, too little in parts; elsewhere too much. Alternately I will frustrate you and lead you astray. I can only say that, at the outset, my intention was otherwise; I sought only clarity and simple conclusions. Now I know the worst—that reasons are out of joint with actions, that my best explanation will be obscure, subtle and unsatisfying, and that the human mind is a tangle of unexplored pathways.

•

"My wife and I decide to separate, and then suddenly we are almost happy together." This is a sentence full of ironies and lies. For example, I call her my wife. Technically this is true. But now that I am leaving, the thought is in both our hearts: "Can a marriage of eleven months really be called a marriage?" Moreover, it was only a civil ceremony, a ten-minute formality performed at the

City Hall by a man who, one could tell, had been drinking heavily over lunch. Perhaps if we had done it in a cathedral surrounded by robed priests intoning Latin benedictions we would not now be falling apart. As we put on our coats to go to the art gallery, I mention this idea to Lucy. "A year," she says. "With Latin we might have lasted a year." We laugh. This is the most courageous statement she has made since we became aware of our defeat, better than all her sour tears. Usually she is too self-conscious to make jokes. Seeing me smile, she blushes and becomes confused, happy to have pleased me, happy to be happy, in the final analysis, happy to be sad because the sadness frees her to be what she could never be before. Like many people, we are both masters of beginnings and endings, but founder in the middle of things. It takes a wise and mature individual to manage that which intervenes, the duration which is a necessary part of life and marriage. So there is a sense in which we are not married, though something *is* ending. And therein lies the greater irony. For in ending, in separating, we are finally and ineluctably together, locked as it were in a ritual recantation. We are going to the art gallery (I am guilty of over-determining the symbol) together.

•

It is winter in Saskatoon, to my mind the best of seasons because it is the most inimical to human existence. The weather forecaster gives the temperature, the wind chill factor and the number of seconds it takes to freeze exposed skin. Driving between towns one remembers to pack a winter survival kit (matches, candle, chocolate, flares, down sleeping bag) in case of a breakdown. Earlier in the week just outside the city limits a man disappeared after setting out to walk a quarter of a mile from one farmhouse to another, swallowed up by the cold prairie night. (This is, I believe, a not unpleasant way to die once the initial period of discomfort has been passed.) Summer in Saskatoon is a collection of minor irritants: heat and dust, blackflies and tent caterpillars, the night-time electrical storms that leave the unpaved concession roads impassable troughs of gumbo mud. But winter has the beauty of a plausible finality. I drive out to the airport early in the morning to watch jets land in a pink haze of ice crystals. During the long nights the *aurora borealis* seems to touch the rooftops. But best of all is the city itself which takes on a kind of ghostliness, a dreamlike quality that combines emptiness (there seem to be so few people) and the mists rising from the heated buildings to produce a mystery. Daily I tramp the paths along the riverbank, crossing and re-crossing the bridges, watching the way the city changes in the pale winter light. Beneath me the unfrozen parts of the river smoke and boil, raging to become still. Winter in Saskatoon is a time of anxious waiting and endurance; all that beauty is alien, a constant threat. Many things do not endure. Our marriage, for example, was vernal, a product of the brief, sweet, prairie spring.

•

Neither Lucy nor I was born here; Mendel came from Russia. In fact there is a feeling of the camp about Saskatoon, the temporary abode. At the university there are photographs of the town—in 1905 there were three frame buildings and a tent. In a bar I nearly came to blows with a man campaigning to preserve a movie theatre built in 1934. In Saskatoon that is ancient history, that is the cave painting at Lascaux. Lucy hails from an even newer settlement in the wild Peace River country where her father went to raise cattle and ended up a truck mechanic. Seven years ago she came to Saskatoon to work in a garment factory (her left hand bears a burn scar from a clothes press). Next fall she begins law school. Despite this evidence of intelligence, determination and ability, Lucy has no confidence in herself. In her mother's eyes she will never measure up, and that is all that is important. I myself am a proud man and a gutter snob. I wear a ring in my left ear and my hair long. My parents migrated from a farm in Wisconsin to a farm in Saskatchewan in 1952 and still drive back every year to see the trees. I am two courses short of a degree in philosophy which I will never receive. I make my living at what comes to hand, house painting when I am wandering; since I settled with Lucy, I've worked as the lone overnight editor at the local newspaper. Against the bosses, I am a union man; against the union, I am an independent. When the publisher asked me to work days, I quit. That was a month ago. That was when Lucy knew I was leaving. Deep down she understands my nature. Mendel is another case: he was a butcher and a man who left traces. Now on the north bank of the river there are giant meat-packing plants spilling forth the odours of death, guts and excrement. Across the street are the holding pens for the cattle and the rail lines that bring them to slaughter. Before building his art gallery Mendel actually kept his paintings in this sprawling complex of buildings, inside the slaughterhouse. If you went to his office, you would sit in a waiting room with a Picasso or a Roualt on the wall. Perhaps even a van Gogh. The gallery is downriver at the opposite end of the city, very clean and modern. But whenever I go there I hear the panicky bellowing of the death-driven steers and see the streams of blood and the carcasses and smell the stench and imagine the poor beasts rolling their eyes at Gauguin's green and luscious leaves as the bolt enters their brains.

•

We have decided to separate. It is a wintry Sunday afternoon. We are going to the Mendel Art Gallery. Watching Lucy shake her hair out and tuck it into her knitted hat, I suddenly feel close to tears. Behind her are the framed photographs of weathered prairie farmhouses, the vigorous spider plants, the scarred child's school desk where she does her studying, the brick-and-board bookshelf with her meagre library. (After eleven months there is still nothing of me that will remain.) This is an old song; there is no gesture of Lucy's that does not fill me instantly with pity, the child's hand held up to deflect the blow, her desperate attempts to conceal unworthiness. For her part she naturally sees me as the father who, in that earlier existence, proved so practised in evasion and flight. The fact that I am now leaving her only reinforces her intuition—it is as if she has expected it all along, almost as if she has been working toward it. This goes to show the force of initial impressions. For example I will never forget the first time I saw Lucy. She was limping across Broadway, her feet swathed in bandages and jammed into her pumps, her face alternately distorted with agony and composed in dignity. I followed her for blocks—

she was beautiful and wounded, the kind of woman I am always looking for to redeem me. Similarly, what she will always remember is that first night we spent together when all I did was hold her while she slept because, taking the bus home, she had seen a naked man masturbating in a window. Thus she had arrived at my door, laughing hysterically, afraid to stay at her own place alone, completely undone. At first she had played the temptress because she thought that was what I wanted. She kissed me hungrily and unfastened my shirt buttons. Then she ran into the bathroom and came out crying because she had dropped and broken the soap dish. That was when I put my arms around her and comforted her, which was what she had wanted from the beginning.

•

An apology for my style: I am not so much apologizing as invoking a tradition. Heraclitus whose philosophy may not have been written in fragments but certainly comes to us in that form. Kierkegaard who mocked Hegel's system-building by writing everything as if it were an afterthought, *The Unscientific Postscript*. Nietzsche who wrote in aphorisms or what he called "attempts," dry runs at the subject matter, even arguing contradictory points of view in order to see all sides. Wittgenstein's *Investigations*, his fragmentary response to the architectonic of the earlier *Tractatus*. Traditional story writers compose a beginning, a middle and an end, stringing these together in continuity as if there were some whole which they represented. Whereas I am writing fragments and discursive circumlocutions about an object that may not be complete or may be infinite. "Dog Attempts to Drown Man in Saskatoon" is my title, cribbed from a facetious newspaper headline. Lucy and I were married because of her feet and because she glimpsed a man masturbating in a window as her bus took her home from work. I feel that in discussing these occurrences, these facts (our separation, the dog, the city, the weather, a trip to the art gallery) as constitutive of a non-system, I am peeling away some of the mystery of human life. I am also of the opinion that Mendel should have left the paintings in the slaughterhouse.

•

The discerning reader will by now have trapped me in a number of inconsistencies and doubtful statements. For example, we are not separating—I am leaving my wife and she has accepted that fact because it reaffirms her sense of herself as a person worthy of being left. Moreover it was wrong of me to pity her. Lucy is a quietly capable woman about to embark on what will inevitably be a successful career. She is not a waif nor could she ever redeem me with her suffering. Likewise she was wrong to view me as forever gentle and forbearing in the sexual department. And finally I suspect that there was more than coincidence in the fact that she spotted the man in his window on my night off from the newspaper. I do not doubt that she saw the man; he is a recurring nightmare of Lucy's. But whether she saw him that particular night, or some night in the past, or whether she made him up out of whole cloth and came to believe in him, I cannot say. About her feet, however, I have been truthful. That day she had just come from her doctor after having the stitches removed.

•

Lucy's clumsiness. Her clumsiness stems from the fact that she was born with six toes on each foot. This defect, I'm sure, had something to do with the way her mother mistreated her. Among uneducated folk there is often a feeling that physical anomalies reflect mental flaws. And as a kind of punishment for being born (and afterwards because her brother had died), Lucy's feet were never looked at by a competent doctor. It wasn't until she was twenty-six and beginning to enjoy a new life that she underwent a painful operation to have the vestigial digits excised. This surgery left her big toes all but powerless; now they flop like stubby, white worms at the ends of her feet. Where she had been a schoolgirl athlete with six toes, she became awkward and ungainly with five.

•

Her mother, Celeste, is one of those women who make feminism

103

a *cause célèbre*—no, that is being glib. Truthfully, she was never any man's slave. I have the impression that after the first realization, the first inkling that she had married the wrong man, she entered into the role of submissive female with a strange, destructive gusto. She seems to have had an immoderate amount of hate in her, enough to spread its poison among the many people who touched her in a kind of negative of the parable of loaves and fishes. And the man, the father, was not so far as I can tell cruel, merely in-effectual, just the wrong man. Once, years later, Lucy and Celeste were riding on a bus together when Celeste pointed to a man sitting a few seats ahead and said, "That is the one I loved." That was all she ever said on the topic and the man himself was a balding, petty functionary type, completely uninteresting except in terms of the exaggerated passion Celeste had invested in him over the years. Soon after Lucy's father married Celeste he realized he would never be able to live with her—he absconded for the army, abandoning her with the first child in a drover's shack on a cattle baron's estate. (From time to time Lucy attempts to write about her childhood—her stories always seem unbelievable—a world of infanticide, blood feuds and brutality. I can barely credit these tales, seeing her so prim and composed, not prim but you know how she sits very straight in her chair and her hair is always in place and her clothes are expensive if not quite stylish and her manners are correct without being at all natural; Lucy is com-posed in the sense of being made up or put together out of pieces, not in the sense of being tranquil. But nevertheless she carries these *cauchemars* in her head: the dead babies found beneath the fencerow, blood on sheets, shotgun blasts in the night, her brother going under the highway roller, her mother's cruel silence.) The father fled as I say. He sent them money orders, three-quarters of his pay, to that point he was responsible. Celeste never spoke of him and his infrequent visits home were always a surprise to the children; his visits and the locked bedroom door and the hot, breathy silence of what went on behind the door; Celeste's rising vexation and hysteria; the new pregnancy; the postmarks on the money orders. Then the boy died. Perhaps he was Celeste's favourite, a perfect one to hold over the tall, already beautiful, monster with six toes and (I conjecture again) her father's look.

104

The boy died and the house went silent—Celeste had forbidden a word to be spoken—and this was the worst for Lucy, the cold parlour circumspection of Protestant mourning. They did not utter a redeeming sound, only replayed the image of the boy running, laughing, racing the machine, then tripping and going under, being sucked under—Lucy did not even see the body, and in an access of delayed grief almost two decades later she would tell me she had always assumed he just flattened out like a cartoon character. Celeste refused to weep; only her hatred grew like a heavy weight against her children. And in that vacuum, that terrible silence accorded all feeling and especially the mysteries of sex and death, the locked door of the bedroom and the shut coffin lid, the absent father and the absent brother, somehow became inextricably entwined in Lucy's mind; she was only nine, a most beautiful monster, surrounded by absent gods and a bitter worship. So that when she saw the naked man calmly masturbating in the upper storey window from her bus, framed as it were under the cornice of a Saskatoon rooming house, it was for her like a vision of the centre of the mystery, the scene behind the locked door, the corpse in its coffin, God, and she immediately imagined her mother waiting irritably in the shadow just out of sight with a towel to wipe the sperm from the windowpane, aroused, yet almost fainting at the grotesque denial of her female passion.

•

Do not, if you wish, believe any of the above. It is psychological jazz written *en marge*; I am a poet of marginalia. Some of what I write is utter crap and wishful thinking. Lucy is not "happy to be sad"; she is seething inside because I am betraying her. Her anger gives her the courage to make jokes; she blushes when I laugh because she still hopes that I will stay. Of course my willingness to accompany her to the art gallery is inspired by guilt. She is completely aware of this fact. Her invitation is premeditated, manipulative. No gesture is lost; all our acts are linked and repeated. She is, after all, Celeste's daughter. Also do not believe for a moment that I hate that woman for what she was. That instant on the bus in a distant town when she pointed out the man she truly loved, she somehow redeemed herself for Lucy and for me, showing herself receptive of forgiveness and pity. Nor do I hate Lucy though I am leaving her.

●

My wife and I decide to separate, and then suddenly we are almost happy together. I repeat this crucial opening sentence for the purpose of reminding myself of my general intention. In a separate notebook next to me (vodka on ice sweating onto and blurring the ruled pages) I have a list of subjects to cover: 1) blindness (the man the dog led into the river was blind); 2) a man I know who was gored by a bison (real name to be withheld); 3) Susan the weaver and her little girl and the plan for us to live in Pelican Narrows; 4) the wolves at the city zoo; 5) the battlefields of Batoche and Duck Lake; 6) bridge symbolism; 7) a fuller description of the death of Lucy's brother; 8) three photographs of Lucy in my possession; 9) my wish to have met Mendel (he is dead) and be his friend; 10) the story of the story or how the dog tried to drown the man in Saskatoon.

●

Call this a play. Call me Orestes. Call her mother Clytemnestra. Her father, the wandering warrior king. (When he died accidentally a year ago, they sent Lucy his diary. Every day of his life he had recorded the weather; that was all.) Like everyone else, we married because we thought we could change one another. I was the brother-friend come to slay the tyrant Celeste; Lucy was to teach me the meaning of suffering. But there is no meaning and in the labyrinth of Lucy's mind the spirit of her past eluded me. Take sex for instance. She is taller than I am; people sometimes think she must be a model. She is without a doubt the most beautiful woman I have been to bed with. Yet there is no passion, no arousal. Between the legs she is as dry as a prairie summer. I am tender, but tenderness is no substitute for biology. Penetration is always painful. She gasps, winces. She will not perform oral sex though sometimes she likes having it done to her, providing she can overcome her embarrassment. What she does love is for me to wrestle her to the living-room carpet and strip her clothes off in a mock rape. She squeals and protests and then scampers naked to the bedroom where she waits impatiently while I get undressed. Only once have I detected her orgasm—this while she sat on my lap fully clothed and I manipulated her with my fingers. It goes without saying she will not talk about these things. She protects herself from herself and there is never any feeling that we are together. When Lucy's periods began, Celeste told her she had cancer. More than once she was forced to eat garbage from a dog's dish. Sometimes her mother would simply lock her out of the house for the night. These stories are shocking; Celeste was undoubtedly mad. By hatred, mother and daughter are manacled together for eternity. "You can change," I say with all my heart. "A woman who only sees herself as a victim never gets wise to herself." "No," she says, touching my hand sadly. "Ah! Ah!" I think, between weeping and words. Nostalgia is form; hope is content. Lucy is an empty building, a frenzy of restlessness, a soul without a future. And I fling out in desperation, Orestes-like, seeking my own Athens and release.

•

More bunk! I'll let you know now that we are not going to the art gallery as I write this. Everything happened some time ago and I am living far away in another country. (Structuralists would characterize my style as "robbing the signifier of the signified." My opening sentence, my premise, is now practically destitute of meaning, or it means everything. Really, this is what happens when you try to tell the truth about something; you end up like the snake biting its own tail. There are a hundred reasons why I left Lucy. I don't want to seem shallow. I don't want to say, well, I was a meat-and-potatoes person and she was a vegetarian, or that I sometimes believe she simply orchestrated the whole fiasco, seduced me, married me, and then refused to be a wife—yes, I would prefer to think that I was guiltless, that I didn't just wander off fecklessly like her father. To explain this, or for that matter to explain why the dog led the man into the river, you have to explain the world, even God—if we accept Gödel's theorem regarding the unjustifiability of systems from within. Everything is a symbol of everything else. Or everything is a symbol of death as Levi-Strauss says. In other words, there is no signified and life is nothing but a long haunting. Perhaps that is all that I am trying to say . . .) However, we *did* visit the art gallery one winter Sunday near the end of our eleven-month marriage. There were two temporary exhibitions and all of Mendel's slaughterhouse pictures had been stored in the basement. One wing was devoted to photographs of grain elevators, very phallic with their little overhanging roofs. We laughed about this together; Lucy was kittenish, pretending to be shocked. Then she walked across the hall alone to contemplate the acrylic prairie-scapes by local artists. I descended the stairs to drink coffee and watch the frozen river. This was downstream from the Idylwyld Bridge where the fellow went in (there is an open stretch of two or three hundred yards where a hot water outlet prevents the river from freezing over completely) and it occurred to me that if he had actually drowned, if the current had dragged him under the ice, they wouldn't have found his body until the spring breakup. And probably they would have discovered it hung up on the weir which I could see from the gallery window.

•

Forget it. A bad picture: Lucy upstairs "appreciating" art, me downstairs thinking of bodies under the ice. Any moment now she will come skipping toward me flushed with excitement after a successful cultural adventure. That is not what I meant to show you. That Lucy is not a person, she is a caricature. When legends are born, people die. Rather let us look at the place where all reasons converge. No. Let me tell you how Lucy is redeemed: preamble and anecdote. Her greatest fear is that she will turn into Celeste. Naturally, without noticing it, she is becoming more and more like her mother every day. She has the financial independence Celeste no doubt craved, and she has been disappointed in love. Three times. The first man made himself into a wandering rage with drugs. The second was an adulterer. Now

108

me. Already she is acquiring an edge of bitterness, of why-me-ness. But, and this is an Everest of a but, the woman can dance! I don't mean at the disco or in the ballroom; I don't mean she studied ballet. We were strolling in Diefenbaker Park one summer day shortly after our wedding (this is on the bluffs overlooking Mendel's meat-packing plant) when we came upon a puppet show. It was some sort of children's fair: there were petting zoos, pony rides, candy stands, bicycles being given away as prizes, all that kind of thing in addition to the puppets. It was a famous troupe which had started in the sixties as part of the counter-culture movement—I need not mention the name. The climax of the performance was a stately dance by two giant puppets perhaps thirty feet tall, a man and a woman, backwoods types. We arrived just in time to see the woman rise from the ground, supported by three puppeteers. She rises from the grass stiffly then spreads her massive arms toward the man and an orchestra begins a reel. It is an astounding sight. I notice that the children in the audience are rapt. And suddenly I am aware of Lucy, her face aflame, this crazy grin and her eyes dazzled. She is looking straight up at the giant woman. The music, as I say, begins and the puppet sways and opens her arms towards her partner (they are both very stern, very grave) and Lucy begins to sway and spread her arms. She lifts her feet gently, one after the other, begins to turn, then swings back. She doesn't know what she is doing; this is completely unselfconscious. There is only Lucy and the puppets and the dance. She is a child again and I am in awe of her innocence. It is a scene that brings a lump to my throat: the high, hot, summer sun, the children's faces like flowers in a sea of grass, the towering, swaying puppets, and Lucy lost in herself. Lucy, dancing. Probably she no longer remembers this incident. At the time, or shortly after, she said, "Oh no! Did I really? Tell me I didn't do that!" She was laughing, not really embarrassed. "Did anyone see me?" And when the puppeteers passed the hat at the end of the show, I turned out my pockets, I gave them everything I had.

•

I smoke Gitanes. I like to drink in an Indian bar on 20th Street near Eaton's. My nose was broken in a car accident when I was eighteen; it grew back crooked. I speak softly; sometimes I stutter. I don't like crowds. In my spare time, I paint large pictures of the city. Photographic realism is my style. I work on a pencil grid using egg tempera because it's better for detail. I do shopping centres, old movie theatres that are about to be torn down, slaughterhouses. While everyone else is looking out at the prairie, I peer inward and record what is merely transitory, what is human. Artifice. Nature defeats me. I cannot paint ripples on a lake, or the movement of leaves, or a woman's face. Like most people, I suppose, my heart is broken because I cannot be what I wish to be. On the day in question, one of the coldest of the year, I hike down from the university along Saskatchewan Drive overlooking the old railway hotel, the modest office blocks, and the ice-shrouded gardens of the city. I carry a camera, snapping end-of-the-world photos for a future canvas. At the Third Avenue Bridge I pause to admire the lattice of I-beams, black against the frozen mist swirling up from the river and the translucent exhaust plumes of the ghostly cars shuttling to and fro. Crossing the street, I descend the wooden steps into Rotary Park, taking two more shots of the bridge at a close angle before the film breaks from the cold. I swing round, focussing on the squat ugliness of the Idylwyld Bridge with its fat concrete piers obscuring the view upriver, and then suddenly an icy finger seems to touch my heart: out on the river, on the very edge of the snowy crust where the turbid waters from the outlet pipe churn and steam, a black dog is playing. I refocus. The dog scampers in a tight circle, races toward the brink, skids to a stop, barks furiously at something in the grey water. I stumble forward a step or two. Then I see the man, swept downstream, bobbing in the current, his arms flailing stiffly. In another instant, the dog leaps after him, disappears, almost as if I had dreamed it. I don't quite know what I am doing, you understand. The river is no man's land. First I am plunging through the knee-deep snow of the park. Then I lose my footing on the bank and find myself sliding on my seat onto the river ice. Before I have time to think, "There is a man in the river," I am sprinting to intercept him, struggling to untangle the camera from around my neck, stripping off my coat. I have forgotten momentarily how long it takes exposed

110

skin to freeze and am lost in a frenzy of speculation upon the impossibility of existence in the river, the horror of the current dragging you under the ice at the end of the open water, the creeping numbness, again the impossibility, the alienness of the idea itself, the dog and the man immersed. I feel the ice rolling under me, throw myself flat, wrapped in a gentle terror, then inch forward again, spread-eagled, throwing my coat by a sleeve, screaming, "Catch it! Catch it!" to the man whirling toward me, scrabbling with bloody hands at the crumbling ledge. All this occupies less time than it takes to tell. He is a strange bearlike creature, huge in an old duffel coat with its hood up, steam rising around him, his face bloated and purple, his red hands clawing at the ice shelf, an inhuman "awing" sound emanating from his throat, his eyes rolling upwards. He makes no effort to reach the coat sleeve trailed before him as the current carries him by. Then the dog appears, paddling toward the man, straining to keep its head above the choppy surface. The dog barks, rests a paw on the man's shoulder, seems to drag him under a little, and then the man is striking out wildly, fighting the dog off, being twisted out into the open water by the eddies. I see the leather hand harness flapping from the dog's neck and suddenly the full horror of the situation assails me: the man is blind. Perhaps he understands nothing of what is happening to him, the world gone mad, this freezing hell. At the same moment, I feel strong hands grip my ankles and hear another's laboured breathing. I look over my shoulder. There is a pink-cheeked policeman with a thin yellow moustache stretched on the ice behind me. Behind him, two teenage boys are in the act of dropping to all fours, making a chain of bodies. A fifth person, a young woman, is running toward us. "He's blind," I shout. The policeman nods: he seems to comprehend everything in an instant. The man in the water has come to rest against a jutting point of ice a few yards away. The dog is much nearer, but I make for the man, crawling on my hands and knees, forgetting my coat. There seems nothing to fear now. Our little chain of life reaching toward the blind drowning man seems sufficient against the infinity of forces which have culminated in this moment. The crust is rolling and bucking beneath us as I take his wrists. His fingers, hard as talons, lock into mine. Immediately he ceases to utter that terrible, unearthly bawling sound. Inching backward, I somehow contrive to lever the dead weight of his body over the ice lip, then drag him on his belly like a sack away from the water. The cop turns him gently on his back; he is breathing in gasps, his eyes rolling frantically. "Tank you. Tank you," he whispers, his strength gone. The others quickly remove their coats and tuck them around the man who now looks like some strange beached fish, puffing and muttering in the snow. Then in the eerie silence that follows, broken only by the shushing sound of traffic on the bridges, the distant whine of a siren coming nearer, the hissing river and my heart beating, I look into the smoky water once more and see that the dog is gone. I am dazed; I watch a drop of sweat freezing on the policeman's moustache. I stare into the grey flux where it slips quietly under the ice and disappears. One of the boys offers me a cigarette. The blind man moans; he says, "I go home now. Dog good. I all right. I walk home." The boys glance at each other. The woman is shivering. Everything seems empty and anticlimactic. We are shrouded in enigma. The policeman takes out a notebook, a tiny symbol of rationality, scribbled words against the void. As an ambulance crew skates a stretcher down the river bank, he begins to ask the usual questions, the usual, unanswerable questions.

•

This is not the story I wanted to tell. I repeat this *caveat* as a reminder that I am willful and wayward as a storyteller, not a good storyteller at all. The right story, the true story, had I been able to tell it, would have changed your life—but it is buried, gone, lost. The next day Lucy and I drive to the spot where I first saw the dog. The river is once more sanely empty and the water boils quietly where it has not yet frozen. Once more I tell her how it happened, but she prefers the public version, what she hears on the radio or reads in the newspaper, to my disjointed impressions. It is also true that she knows she is losing me and she is at the stage where it is necessary to deny strenuously all my values and perceptions. She wants to think that I am just like her father or that I always intended to humiliate her. The facts of the case are that the man and dog apparently set out to cross the Idylwyld Bridge but turned off along the approach and walked into the water, the man a little ahead of the dog. In the news account, the dog is accused of insanity, dereliction of duty and a strangely uncanine malevolence. "Dog Attempts to Drown Man," the headline reads. Libel law prevents speculation or the human victim's mental state, his intentions. The dog is dead, but the tone is jocular. *Dog Attempts to Drown Man*. All of which means that no one knows what happened from the time the man stumbled off the sidewalk on Idylwyld to the time he fell into the river and we are free to invent structures and symbols as we see fit. The man survives, it seems, his strange baptism, his trial by cold and water. I know in my own mind that he appeared exhausted, not merely from the experience of near-drowning, but from before, in spirit, while the dog seemed eager and alert. We know, or at least we can all agree to theorize, that a bridge is a symbol of change (one side to the other, hence death), of connection (the marriage of opposites), but also of separation from the river of life, a bridge is an object of culture. Perhaps man and dog chose together to walk through the pathless snows to the water's edge and throw themselves into uncertainty. The man was blind as are we all; perhaps he sought illumination in the frothing waste. Perhaps they went as old friends. Or perhaps the dog accompanied the man only reluctantly, the man forcing the dog to lead him across the ice. I saw the dog swim to him, saw the man fending the dog off. Perhaps the dog was trying to save its master, or perhaps it was only playing, not understanding in the least what was happening. Whatever is the case my allegiance is with the dog; the man is too human, too predictable. But man and dog together are emblematic—that is my impression at any rate—they are the mind and spirit, the one blind, the other dumb; one defeated, the other naive and hopeful, both forever going out. And I submit that after all the simplified explanations and crude jokes about the blind man and his dog, the act is full of a strange and terrible mystery, of beauty.

•

My wife and I decide to separate, and then suddenly we are almost happy together. But this was long ago, as was the visit to the Mendel Art Gallery and my time in Saskatoon. And though the moment when Lucy is shaking down her hair and tucking it into her knitted cap goes on endlessly in my head as does the reverberation of that other moment when the dog disappears under the ice, there is much that I have already forgotten. I left Lucy because she was too real, too hungry for love, while I am a dreamer. There are two kinds of courage: the courage that holds things together and the courage that throws them away. The first is more common; it is the cement of civilization; it is Lucy's. The second is the courage of drunks and suicides and mystics. My sign is impurity. By leaving, you understand, I proved that I was unworthy. I have tried to write Lucy since that winter—her only response has been to return my letters unopened. This is appropriate. She means for me to read them myself, those tired, clotted apologies. I am the writer of the words; she knows well enough they are not meant for her. But my words are sad companions and sometimes I remember . . . well . . . the icy water is up to my neck and I hear the ghost dog barking, she tried to warn me; yes, yes, I say, but I was blind.

Fire Drill

The bentwood rocker in our living-room belonged to Aunt Maggie. Jack refinished it, glued the joints solid and had the wicker seat re-woven for our third anniversary. But Aunt Maggie died of Alzheimer's Disease, and sitting in her chair always gives me the creepy feeling I'll turn out the same. "You're weirder than I thought," says Jack, eyeing me as if my worst fears have already been realized.

Also in the living-room we have an iron wood-burning stove of the kind Jack sells out of his bicycle shop over the winter lull, and a giant aquarium which I gave him as a graduation present. The aquarium is full of greenish water, plastic plants and coloured pebbles, but the last Black Molly vanished six years ago when we moved to Aurora from Toronto. For a while it housed a goldfish Erin won at the county fair, but no one has seen "Gilda" for months. Now Erin perches on the landing above the tank and throws in pennies for wishes. We're the only family I know with a private wishing well in the living-room. I tell Jack he's pretty weird himself.

On Erin's first day of kindergarten I forget what I'm doing and sit in Aunt Maggie's chair by mistake. Erin huddles in my lap, pale as death, unwilling to cry, taut as piano wire. I don't know which of us is freaked out the most. Erin is freaked out because they pulled a surprise fire drill on her bus on the way home and it terrified her. I'm freaked out because Erin is freaked out. But except for landing in Aunt Maggie's rocker I am maintaining control.

I am waiting for Jack to get home from the shop before I break down completely. This is as per my instructions from our therapist who has deduced that I am unable to cope well in crisis situations. Now, if anything happens to Erin, I keep my lips zipped up, calmly hand her over to her father, and leave the room. Later, when the cut is cleaned and bandaged, when the bruise is kissed and the tears wiped away, she can come to me for a hug. The therapist says this way I won't turn my daughter into a basket case before she gets to high school.

Naturally, I have already phoned Jack.

"Come right home," I say. "I can't handle it. She won't say a word. They stopped the bus in the middle of the road and made all the kids climb out the back. She didn't know what was happening."

"She'll be okay," says Jack. He is altogether too cool in a crisis. A year ago I nearly died hemorrhaging from an ectopic pregnancy. The orderlies were wheeling me into the operating room, my abdomen full of blood, tubes sprouting from my arms and nose, and someone whispers, "Has the husband seen her? Make sure she sees her husband before she goes under." I know this is the end. I know I'm going to check out on the table. Jack bends over me, and I realize we have to make the most of this last moment together. He says, "How does it feel to have one of those things down your nose?" I say, "Well, it's not as bad as you might think." Those were my last words. At least, they could have been my last words. As I say, Jack is altogether too cool.

"How do you know she'll be okay? You can't see her. Why would they scare a kid like that?"

"It's the law," he says. "They do it for their own protection."

"It's a dumb law."

This is the first time I have put Erin in the hands of an institution, except for the dismal two months she spent in hospital when she was three. On that occasion we rushed her to Emergency with

116

an acute asthma attack. The doctors had to do a tracheotomy, then misplaced and fouled the hole, scarring her throat. For a while we thought we were going to lose her. I even told Jack to call a priest. We were waiting outside surgery, expecting the worst, and no priest showed up. I was sobbing, trembling, leaning on Jack to stay upright, when finally a nurse appeared and said Erin was all right. "Where's the damn priest?" I asked Jack. That was the first thing I thought of. "You didn't call the priest, did you?" Jack just looked sheepish.

After that experience, I can't stand the thought of anything happening to Erin. I won't let anyone but Jack or my mother touch her. I write down the licence numbers of speeding cars and phone the police. I keep my eye on suspicious-looking strangers, noting significant physical characteristics in case I have to give a description. My ears are tuned to the sound of her voice when she rides her bicycle down the block out of sight. And in my nightmares, I am continually running to save her from drowning or from blazing buildings.

"I think I'll stay home from school tomorrow," she says, echoing my thoughts. She utters the words in a matter-of-fact, adult manner, mimicking Jack when he takes a day off work.

"We'll see what Daddy says," I reply. Despite a flurry of broody emotions, I am able to think clearly that the therapist would not want me to make a decision on this without consulting my husband.

Later, when he reaches home, we're calmer.

"There," he says. "Erin's okay. You're the one who gets upset."

"We thought there was a real fire on the bus," I say. "We don't want to go to school tomorrow."

Jack shakes his head. He feels as if he has to take responsibility for the whole family. Sometimes he feels as if he's got two kids and no wife. And I have to admit there is some truth to that, though it wasn't always so. It is just that after Erin's hospital fiasco and my bad pregnancy, I've never had a chance to catch up. Three months ago Jack and I stopped having sex and started counselling. For Jack, this is no substitute. When I turned thirty in July, he told our bowling buddies, "She's hitting her prime now. I don't know how long I'll be able to keep up these outside activities now that Jenny's over the big three-oh." He said it nicely; Jack loves me. But his voice had a sad ring to it which made me want to cry. "You're afraid of taking action," says our therapist, with her usual flair for the obvious. "You're afraid of the consequences of taking steps."

After supper, notable only for the overcooked cauliflower and our silence, he takes Erin upstairs to her bedroom for one of their heart-to-hearts. She has always told Jack more than she tells me. I interrupt and give advice. I try to tell her how to handle situations that I couldn't handle when I was her age. When she tells me about the fire drill, I immediately empathize. "Were you scared, honey? You shouldn't have been scared. It was only a drill." She stops talking and looks depressed. I have failed to say the right words.

My husband never falls into that trap. He just lets her talk. He says, "Is that right?" or "And then what happened?" And after a while she's explained things to herself and becomes quiet. Then he says, "Well, that's the way the world works, Erin." It's a little infuriating. I try and screw up; Jack does nothing and has a somewhat mature relationship with our daughter. After they have had one of these talks, they both look at me as if I were the witless child caught up in a whirl of infantile fears and feelings.

On this particular night, they come solemnly down the stairs to the landing and Jack pulls a penny out of his pocket and hands it to Erin.

"Here we go," he says. "You remember the words?"

"I wish I wouldn't be afraid of that pesky old fire drill again," she says, enunciating slowly, tossing the coppery new penny into the aquarium.

I glare at Jack. He gets away with cheap tricks like that because he doesn't get excited. Sometimes, I tell the therapist, I think he doesn't care as much as I do. If he cared, he wouldn't be able to think clearly either, right?

Erin and I are alike in this: we both believe in magic doors, talking animals and rewards for the virtuous. When Peter Pan saves Tinker Bell by asking the audience if it believes in fairies, I nod my head just as vigorously as Erin does, shaking the tears out of my eyes. We are dreamers, we like to sift among the possibilities.

The next day on her way out the door to catch her bus, she asks, "What are you going to do all morning without me?"

"Oh, I'll make out," I say. "I'll find something."

She's wearing a dress she picked out herself. It has a white skirt with black piping, a gray bodice and a white Dutch collar. It's a little formal for kindergarten, I think, but this is her way of establishing distance from me. As she disappears into the yellow and black bus, as the doors accordion shut behind her, all I can think of is how I used to fan her butt with my hair dryer when she got diaper rash. Frankly, I don't know what I'll do all morning.

Then Jack calls. He's decided we're out of shape. Now that Erin's in school and we have all this free time, he wants me to sign up for morning Nautilus workouts with him. He sounds enthusiastic, but I know Jack is not worried about physical fitness. What he really means is that he doesn't want me to turn neurotic on him, sitting around the house thinking about fire drills. To tell the truth, I'm relieved. I say yes, giving the impression of psychological normalcy.

After I hang up, I drive into town and buy myself a workout suit, dance slippers, sweat socks, a sport bra and a pralines and peach cone at Baskin-Robbins. Then I break the speed limit twice on my way home to be there when Erin arrives. I am sitting on the steps in my new outfit when she alights from the bus.

Grim. I say to myself, "Children are not supposed to look this unhappy." As she drags across the street, I jog out to the picket fence to meet her. I made Jack build this fence to keep Erin in and protect her from dogs and perverts. My fingers are in my mouth, and for a brief, paranoiac moment, I tell myself she is blaming all this on me. Kindergarten was invented by mothers who want to get rid of their babies, right?

"How was school?" I ask.

"Okay," says Erin, without looking at me. She trudges into the yard, lugging her school bag like a ball and chain.

"Was the bus ride okay?" I ask. I want a conversation here. I want her to know I care. But somehow I feel like the Wicked Witch of the North harassing Judy Garland along the Yellow Brick Road.

"Yes," she moans.

I know something has happened. Right away I want to pry it out of her.

"What's the matter, sweetheart?" I ask like a fool, scrunching down on the cement walk so that our faces are on the same level. Why does it seem to stab me that she will not make eye contact? I fight the hysteria rising in my chest like water in a clogged sink, feeling as though any move I might make will only increase her burden.

"We had a pretend fire drill at school," she says, adding quickly, "I wasn't afraid as much as yesterday. They didn't ring the fire thing."

"The siren," I say.

She ignores me.

"Tomorrow we're going to have a real fire drill and the teacher will time us with a real watch. The teacher said we have to be fast because slowpokes can die in a fire."

I don't know what to say. I send my child to kindergarten and right off the bat they are instilling a morbid and abnormal obsession with fire hazards. Two days ago she was a carefree urchin with a tracheotomy scar in her throat to remind me of her utter fragility, and this morning she's a short adult striving to deal with the stress of unpredictable and incomprehensible death threats. Twenty years from now she'll have cancer from this.

"Twenty years from now she'll have cancer," I tell Jack over the phone. "I don't think our child will ever laugh again."

"It seems a little excessive," says Jack. "But they probably know what they're doing. What if there was a real fire?"

"Jack," I say, "have you ever heard of a child dying in a school fire? The school is built of bricks. It can't burn. They are doing this to break her spirit. They don't have to scare the hell out of her the first week."

As usual, Jack refuses to become excited. He refuses to leave the shop early. He claims he has a customer waiting. When I get off the phone, Erin is slumped in Aunt Maggie's chair, her skirt rucked up to her hips, staring at the aquarium.

I am uncomfortably reminded of my own childhood as she tips the rocker back and forth awkwardly with the toe of her shoe. Aunt Maggie came to live with us when I was eight after Uncle Bart was killed in a car accident. She was already a little bughouse even then, though she lived another fifteen years, rocking away, always moving, never getting anywhere. At first I thought she was kindly disposed toward me because she was always taking my hands, kissing them, holding them against her cheek and saying, "Poor little Jenny. Poor little Jenny." But then one day she lifted two of my playmates onto her lap as she rocked and whispered into their ears, thanking them for coming around to visit me so often. "Why are you thanking us?" Michelle Laforte asked. "Well, you know," said Aunt Maggie, conspiratorially, "poor Jenny's a little retarded." Even after I went to university, Aunt Maggie couldn't shake the notion that I was mentally deficient.

That evening, when Erin has gone to bed, Jack leads me gently toward the living-room couch and says, "Let's talk about it." Jack has really gotten into this therapy stuff. He loves the ritualized conversations. Mostly because he always comes off so well. I'm the one who goes ape when Erin scrapes her elbow. I'm the one who refuses to have sex. During one session with the therapist, I exploded. "You don't care, you bastard. When our daughter was dying, you read back issues of *Maclean's*." He looked at me. "That's not true," he said. "When I went outside, when I went to meet your mother at the airport, I cried so hard I couldn't stand up." "Well, why didn't you do that in front of me?" I asked. "Jack realizes he has to take charge," said the therapist. "He has to set an example."

This time, as Jack tries to push me down on the couch (he generally sits in Aunt Maggie's rocker), I say, "I don't want to talk. I want to be alone. I want to go to the basement to do my laundry, and I don't want you interrupting me."

Jack takes this in stride. He understands that we both need alone time. According to my best friend Peggy, who has a crush on him, Jack is the Perfect Husband. This is in contrast to her own husband who chases younger women and embarrasses her at parties. Jack is unfailingly loyal, polite and considerate. The harshest thing he's ever said about our lack of a sex life is "This is your only time around, Jenny. In twenty years you may regret that you wasted it."

While I separate the clothes and start the wash cycle, I think things over. I do not understand why I have lost my sense of proportion. It has something to do with seeing my baby suffering, sinking toward death, butchered by a surgeon who didn't even know her name. (Jack held her in his arms for six straight hours the night she was not supposed to pull through. I was too hysterical to do anything but sob and moan at the foot of her hospital crib.) Now everything that goes wrong immediately escalates in my head to that level of disaster. I am always expecting the worst, believing that things will not turn out well.

We have a store-room next to the laundry, and for a while I rummage in there, examining the leftover paraphernalia of Erin's babyhood. We have kept everything so that we could use it for her brothers and sisters. The automatic swing no longer works when I wind it up. The Big Bird doll we bought when she was three months old is losing its stuffing. In a box in the corner, I find the shipment of baby clothes my sister sent only to have them arrive after Erin had already outgrown them. Her own things are as good as new, neatly folded away in a trunk that smells of mothballs and cedar. Unaccountably, the mothball smell makes me start to cry. Even as I stand here, it says, everything is moving backward and away from me. I am powerless to stop the flow. I realize suddenly that I am terrified and don't know where to turn.

The next morning Erin has a difficult time waking up. She dips her elbow in her Fruit & Fibre, throws a tantrum when I put on her green corduroy jumper, and kicks me in the chin by accident as I buckle her shoes. I shove her out the door as fast as I can, suppressing the urge to motivate her with a hard slap on the rump. Then I peep out the window while she waits, both hands clasped on her school bag, eyes downcast, examining the crumbling edge of the pavement.

Her first day of school already seems a decade away, I think, as I recall Jack posing us for the camera. Snapping shots of Erin and me on the porch, Erin halfway to the gate, three-quarters of the way, Erin slipping through the gate, her hand waving like a flag above the shut gate, me gazing after her, hugging myself in the morning chill. The last photo, when it comes back from the developer, will be a shot of the bus with two tiny feet waiting patiently on the other side for the doors to open. And it is the same now. The last thing I see of Erin is her feet.

"We were not happy this morning," I tell Jack when he comes home from his free earlybird trial at Nautilus. His hair is hanging over his forehead making him look a little like Bobby Kennedy. I'd like to give him a hug, but from previous experience I know that any move in that direction can lead to trouble. Jack will think I want to make love and, when I tell him I won't, his feelings will be hurt.

"We weren't aware that school would be every day," I say. "We thought we could just go when we felt like it."

Jack is eating granola out of the box with his fingers which I hate because he leaves granola crumbs wherever he's been.

"Why do you always say 'we' when you talk about Erin?" he asks. He sounds exactly like the therapist, neither aggressive nor critical, merely curious.

"It's so that, if she happens to overhear, she won't think I'm talking behind her back," I say, my cheeks beginning to burn.

"Oh," he says, flipping the radio dial to a country and western station he likes. Usually he's already gone to the shop this time of day, but the bicycle business takes a seasonal slump as soon as school starts so he's not that worried about opening early. "But she's not in the house."

I feel as if he's trying to get at me now. Using 'we' when I talk about Erin is just a habit, I think. It grew out of consideration for her. But Jack is making a big deal out of it, while pretending not to.

Willie Nelson comes on singing the theme music for *The Electric Horseman* which is Jack's favourite movie and when it's over Jack wanders out the door and heads for work, humming to himself. I am furious with him, but there seems to be no logical way to engage him. Sometimes I just want to throw plates. But Jack never gets mad, so throwing plates would only make me look silly. The fact that I can't make Jack angry almost drives me crazy.

I run upstairs and curl up on the bed with a pillow over my face. What I really want is to call the school and ask them to cancel the fire drill, maybe even excuse Erin so she can come home and play with me. I imagine her rushing terrified for the exit, the warning bells clanging, sirens whooping, her head full of nameless fears, dreaming the smell of smoke, the dart of flames, the screams of other children, while her teacher remorselessly counts off the seconds on her wrist watch. I imagine my baby tripping, stumbling under the hurrying feet, coming to in a hospital, her tiny body making barely a dent in the tight white bedsheets. I feel weak, quivery, yet strangely full of energy.

I head downstairs to the kitchen and pick up the phone.

"I'd like to place a classified ad," I say to the person at the other end. "One large, freshwater aquarium," I say. "Completely equipped. Cheap. Just put that in." In the distance, I hear the wails of fire engine sirens. I dial the shop, hang up. "Do you love me, Jack?" I ask the air.

I remember the house off-campus where Jack lived in his senior year and the year after graduation. It contained a half-dozen boys, almost indistinguishable at first with their long hair and racing bikes, a glade of thriving marijuana plants, a Nixon poster taped to the toilet lid, and eight aquariums. The one I gave Jack was the biggest. Nights they'd turn off the lights and get stoned watching the fish in the green glow of the tanks. I remember the green glow and the bubble patterns on my skin the first time we made love. Daydreaming, I plug in the aquarium and switch on the air pump and underwater light. I am relieved to see that everything is still in working condition.

Watching the slow rise of bubbles, I think how empty the tank is without a live fish fanning its tail amongst the fake water weeds. There is never enough life, I think, and I feel a sudden urge to fill aquariums with minnows, houses with children. When I get down in the dumps, as likely as not, Jack will say something pithy such as: "Life is crap—and then you die." He thinks he's a realist; he scored an A in Atheism in his junior year. But, secretly, I believe, he too is aware of the sad mystery of existence, this brief haunting like the flash of light on a fin or the accelerating rise of a bubble that can't seem to wait to crash to the surface and disappear.

Outside, I hear the metallic screech of the bus brakes. I reach to switch off the aquarium, then decide to leave it. I wait on the couch, bracing myself for what's to come. The gate swings and creaks on its hinges. Erin's feet thud on the steps.

"Hi," I say. "Howdy stranger." I wave my hand, feel silly. Why do I act like such a kid with my kid?

"Hi," she says. She slumps next to me, then falls sideways and nestles her head in my lap.

"Did you have the fire drill?" I ask, aiming to sound light and conversational.

She nods, her chin gouging my stomach.

"Well, a real fire will be no problem after this."

"Mommy, there was a real fire," she says patiently. "A bad boy set fire to the dumpster when we were lining up to go back in."

It occurs to me that I have discovered a new natural law: things always get worse. I resist an impulse to call Jack so that he can participate in this conversation. Since I am holding her and she is talking and her limbs are moving, even I can see she is unhurt. Physically. But my nightmares are coming true. In kindergarten my baby is falling under an evil sign. She is consorting with sadists and pyromaniacs.

"I closed my eyes in the smoke," she adds. She measures her words as if she is not quite sure how much to tell me. In her face I read the message: Don't fall apart, Mommy. Listen. Let me rest. "A little girl started to cry, and I held her hand. I told her, 'You'll be safe if we hold hands.' But I was scared."

I bite my lip and pull her tight against my chest. "That was very brave of you," I say, though I have a lump in my throat. I find it difficult to imagine anyone being little in relation to Erin, this pint-sized shadow self I created.

She's weeping now, letting go after the tension and fatigue of the morning, her tiny hands clasping my waist, her blue-veined throat pulsing next to the shiny tracheotomy scar. To me she still smells like a baby.

In my mind's eye, I picture the two children, hand in hand, standing to one side as the fire trucks spin out their hoses and men deal with the smouldering dumpster. Other children clot together in fear and confusion or race up and down shrieking in mock panic. Teachers pace, smoking cigarettes, making jokes and checking their watches. Erin and her friend bend together, whispering over their knuckle-white hands. Already, I think, she is bringing new life into her world.

At length, I realize that I am the only one crying and that Erin is breathing quietly, dozing. I wake her, slipping off her shoes, stretching her out on the cushions.

She says, "I'm all right, Mommy. The teacher said we would be on TV. Wake me up when it's time, okay?"

125

I drape a blanket over her, then go to the kitchen extension. I call the newspaper and cancel my aquarium ad. Then dictate another: "One antique bentwood rocker. Extremely cheap."

I dial the shop. I say, "Sweetheart, the baby's asleep. She's taking a nap. If you come right home, we can get in a quickie before she wakes up. I can't promise—"

"I'll be right there," says Jack, hanging up before I have a chance to reconsider.

Retracing my steps, I kiss Erin's forehead. Asleep, she is rebuilding her defences, growing stronger. But she will always have a good heart. There will always be this little girl inside.

Heading upstairs to take a shower, I pause on the landing and fish a pocketful of change out of my pants. I toss it into Jack's aquarium, splashing drops of water onto the hardwood floor. As I watch the shoal of pennies, nickels, dimes and quarters slice haphazardly toward the pebble bottom, I cross my fingers. I make a wish.